THE ZONDERLING

Kersti Niebruegge

Kersti Niebruegge
New York

This is a work of fiction. Names, characters, places, and incidents are either a product of the author's imagination or used fictitiously. Any resemblance to actual persons, living or dead, events, or locales is entirely coincidental.

Cover design and photos by Kersti Niebruegge.
Artwork by Kersti Niebruegge.

ISBN (paperback): 978-0-9908710-3-3
ISBN (Kindle eBook): 978-0-9908710-4-0

Library of Congress Control Number: 2015916016

First Edition
November 2015

For New York City.
I love you. I hate you.
I hate you. I love you.
(But you get it. Cool? Cool.)

FLOOR PLANS

The Zonderling

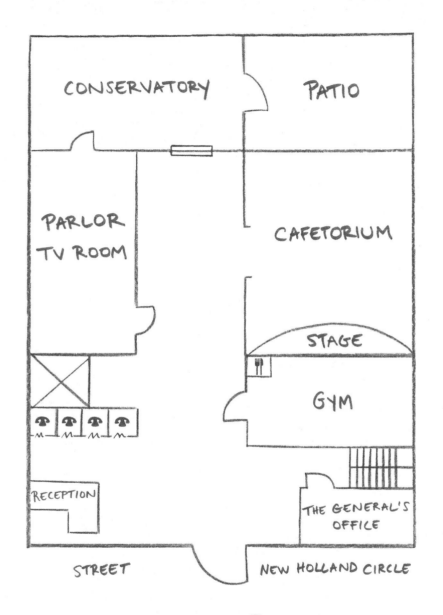

GROUND FLOOR

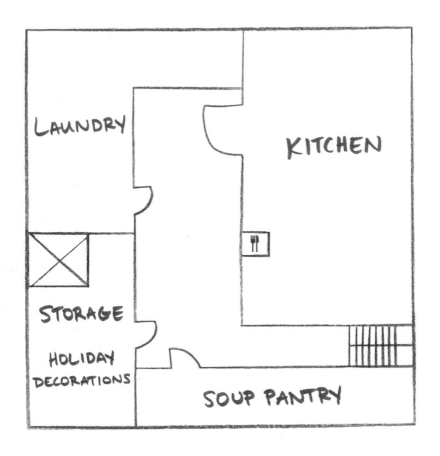

LAUNDRY

KITCHEN

STORAGE

HOLIDAY
DECORATIONS

SOUP PANTRY

BASEMENT

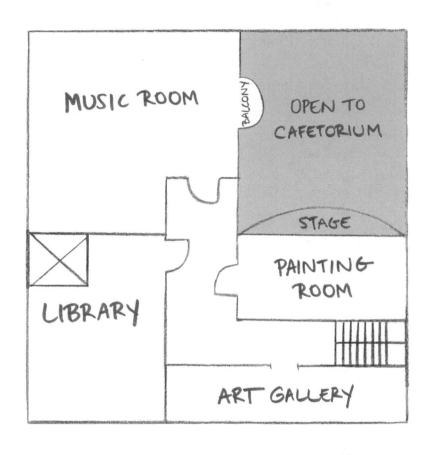

MUSIC ROOM

BALCONY

OPEN TO CAFETORIUM

STAGE

PAINTING ROOM

LIBRARY

ART GALLERY

SECOND FLOOR

ONE

Everyone at the tiny airport in Poubelle, Wisconsin, stared at the preseason football game playing on TV—everyone except for twenty-seven-year-old Heather Baumhauer and her parents, Jim and Sally. Well, maybe Jim was too.

"I don't understand why you're wasting your brand-new master's degree by being a temp in New York," Sally said—for about the millionth time.

"Because it's *New York*, not Wisconsin," Heather said—also for about the millionth time.

"You'll never get a good job. There are already over eight million people there!"

"I have an appointment with a temp agency." *Which you know*, Heather thought. "They staff all the big international companies."

"But you could work for your dad—"

"I'm not going to spreadsheet my life away in snowmobile insurance." Heather turned to her dad. "No offense, Dad."

He wasn't paying attention on account of the TV being on and the Packers being on that TV.

"Uncle Don would love if you continued tending bar at his lodge."

"How does *that* not qualify as wasting my master's?"

"Because you're—"

"Spending all day at the Crappie Lodge and Resort pretending to believe tall tales about the Great Kinockina Lake Musky."

"Heather! Shame on you! You know that my brother's wife's sister's husband's best friend's snowplower has seen the Great Kinockina Lake Musky! It was on—"

"The ten p.m. news!" Heather said, mimicking her mom. She was so sick of stories about a bigger-than-life fish that existed in pretty much all Northwoods fishing communities. The Great Kinockina Lake Musky was the most famous fish in all of La Jolie County. It was always "this big" and "the one that got away." By this point exaggeration had the Great Kinockina Lake Musky about the size of a Green Bay linebacker. Stories about the epic fish began with French Canadian explorers, which would make this specific musky approximately 170 years old if anyone were counting. But no one was ever counting, especially not Sally Baumhauer.

"I can't wait to go somewhere where people can think of other news besides monster fish," Heather said. She gestured toward the drinking fountain. "Christina said that they even have different names for bubblers."

"Uff da! You can't just make up words. How can a bubbler not be a bubbler?"

"I don't know, but it's *New York*."

"Your cousin doesn't know what she's talking about."

"I want to meet people who grew up outside of La Jolie County!"

"Your father's new assistant is from Kenosha," Sally offered. "That's basically Chicago."

"I want to ride a train."

"You rode a train at the zoo."

"A train for *kids*. I can't even fit inside anymore."

"You still rode a train!" For Sally, if something was close enough, then it always counted as the real experience. When she talked about eating the best spaghetti of her life in Italy, she really meant EPCOT Italy.

"I want to eat at a Jewish deli!"

"Well..." Sally said, thinking hard. "Oh, Grundmann's Supper Club! They serve potato pancakes at the Friday fish fry. So there you go!"

"Come on!"

"It's pretty close so long as you don't look at the big Jesus painting behind the cash register," Sally argued. Grundmann's had so much religious paraphernalia in the waiting area that it looked like a Lutheran church exploded within a seven-foot radius of Janet Grundmann's hostess stand. Even Pastor Frannie thought it was a bit much.

"They might have potato pancakes, but Grundmann's certainly doesn't have any real New York bagels," Heather said.

Hearing talk of exotic New York Jewish food was enough to momentarily distract Jim from the game. He shouted over his shoulder, "Don't forget to send me some of that babka stuff. Both chocolate and cinnamon. I wanna know why Elaine kept complaining to Jerry about a lesser babka."

"That reminds me! Snacks!" Sally lifted two handfuls of cheese-curd snack packs from her Mary Poppins–like purse. She kneeled down and stuffed them into Heather's bags.

"Mom! There's no more room for cheese curds! Not after you shoved in all the granola bars last night."

"Don't be silly," Sally said. "See how it squishes?"

"That's so gross."

"And remember to call when you get to Christina's. She knows when you're coming, right? It's too dangerous to stand on the curb alone."

"The Central Park jogger was a million years ago!"

With one swift move, Sally shoved the last cheese pack into the bag, closed the zipper, and bolted upright. "You do *not* go into Central Park alone!"

"Stop watching *Law & Order* reruns!"

"Ripped from the headlines!"

"From twenty years ago!"

Jim turned around. "Sally, where's—"

"Jim, tell her! There was an episode of *Dateline*!"

4

"What?" He didn't know what she was talking about, on account of a game being on TV and him not paying attention. He'd turned around because there was a commercial break and he was looking for the bathroom.

"And remember that *Eye to Eye with Connie Chung* with the girl—"

"What are you even talking about, Mom?"

"Mob debt!"

"Sally," Jim said. "The Wrights went to New York last year, and the only thing that was stolen was their spot in the brunch line."

"Jim—"

"New York is completely safe."

Heather angrily punched the buzzer on a Manhattan apartment building that was next to a greasy kebab takeout. Teens walking home from school, general foot traffic, and a marauding band of indignant pigeons filled the noisy street. She continued to jab the buzzer as she took out her phone. There were already two missed calls from her mom and a text that said, "Study I are?" Texting was not her mom's forte, so Heather assumed this was an autocorrected message that probably meant something like, "Are you OK?" Heather made a call, but not to her mom.

"Christina, where are you? I'm here, and your apartment manager won't let me in. Even though I know he can see me!" She irately waved to the sixty-one-year-old manager who was sitting inside in his drab, cluttered office. Without looking up, the manager pointed to a "Back in 15" sign as he drew hearts on a thick file folder while eating a massive tuna sandwich.

Heather turned around in frustration and unintentionally made eye contact with a bike messenger. While eye contact was considered polite in nearly all other areas of America, Heather had yet to learn that no one made eye contact with strangers in New York unless it was at a cocktail party involving mini grilled cheese on a stick. No eye contact eliminated the constant threat of engaging with people, like construction workers testing reactions to new slang words for *boobs*, or aspiring comedians shooting man-on-the-street videos. As a matter of self-preservation, the MO of all New Yorkers was no eye contact and no smiling. Since no one told Heather about this very important rule, she made a rookie mistake of making eye contact with a human being who was speaking to her.

"Syphilis!" the bike messenger guy screamed as soon as his gaze connected with Heather's. He pointed at Heather. "That whore gave me syphilis!"

Heather froze. Her mom's favorite crime stats began spinning through her head. She whispered into her phone, "Christina, don't tell my mom that she was right about New York." Heather hung up and yelled to the guy. "It's OK! I didn't take your spot in line at the kebab place!"

"Whore!"

At that moment the door to the apartment opened as a resident exited the building. Heather seized the opportunity and rushed into the lobby.

The manager froze midbite of tuna when he noticed her standing inside. Heather saw that the glass door to his office was open. They stared at each other for a second, and then both bolted toward the open door. As the manager tried to shut it, smearing tuna on the glass in the process, Heather wedged herself between the door and the frame.

"Can you please let me into my cousin's place? Christina Baumhauer?" Heather begged. She noticed the nameplate on his desk and thought maybe he'd appreciate the friendliness of her using his name. "Please, Larry, I can't wait for her outside," Heather said.

Ignoring her, Larry continued to press the door against her and eat the remainder of his messy sandwich. Heather gestured toward the street. "I think there's a *crazy* person out there," she said earnestly. "He might be on *drugs*."

Suddenly Larry realized that he really, really had to take a leak. He had been hoping to wear down Heather by holding the door longer than she could withstand, but a war of attrition wasn't going to work for him this time. He prided himself on being able to win any war of attrition, kind of like World War I military generals. Or his mom.

In a last-ditch attempt, Larry pressed the door harder against Heather, hoping she'd leave. He estimated he only had three minutes to spare. He'd had a lot of beer for lunch. Annoyed, he shoved the last piece of tuna into his mouth.

"Baumhauer?" he said, spraying tuna everywhere. "She disappeared days ago."

"Oh no! What happened? Was she on the curb alone? Should I really not do that?"

"Who knows? Sold all of her stuff. Spent it all on some around-the-world or where-in-the-world or whatever-in-the-world airplane ticket."

"OMG!" Heather said, excited. "Is she on a new Carmen Sandiego reality show? Or one of those worldwide race shows?"

Larry's face dropped. Then it quickly filled with anger. "A Mexican's hosting a reality show now?" Larry was furious. "They're taking all our jobs. I can't win! There go my chances on *Win a Sugar Daddy*."

"*You* want to be on a dating show?"

Taking advantage of Heather's confusion, Larry angrily pushed her out of the doorway and locked the door behind him. Through the glass Heather watched him pick up the folder on which he'd been drawing hearts and toss it into the trash. It was labeled, "Sugar Daddy Application."

Suddenly the bike messenger pounded on the building's locked glass door and screamed, "Yo, syphilis bitch! Gimme a condom so I can screw my sister!"

Heather's heart raced. She had nowhere to go. She had no money. She had no return airplane ticket.

She quietly knocked on the manager's office. "Excuse me. Can you recommend any apartments with affordable rent? Somewhere where I won't end up selling crack in Harlem to pay off my debt to the mob? I'd rather not prove my mom right."

Larry swigged from a bottle of sparkling wine as he became more and more depressed. He wanted to be on *Win a Sugar Daddy* so badly. Well, he wanted to be on television really badly. And if he could be on TV *and* get women to make out with him all day long, even better. He deserved to be on TV! He was a successful businessman. He was very handsome (according to the many voice mails left by his mother). And he owned a two-bedroom apartment that he'd earned after many profitable years as a landlord who regularly quadrupled rent every thirteen months. Most people would call his place gaudy, but he knew they were just jealous of his expensive Italian-sports-car-branded furnishings.

What more could those TV producers want? Carmela San Francisco, apparently, Larry thought. *Middle-aged white men need not apply.* He began cleaning out all the *Sugar Daddy*-related audition gear from his office.

As Larry boxed up his roses, tuxedo, bow-and-arrow set, and an archery target, Heather sat with her laptop on the dirty floor of the apartment lobby, with her back against Larry's office. He hadn't given her any helpful apartment information, but he did give her his Wi-Fi password: *5ugardaddy.*

Heather didn't know where to begin, so she typed the words *cheap, clean, apartment,* and *women* into her search engine. She scrolled through the results and was horrified as she read the listings that included headlines like: "Cheap rent! $600 for female roommate who will cook in heels and underwear. CENTRAL PARK WEST!" or "Great location, cheap rent, premium cable included! Only $750 for female roommate who will clean in a Katniss costume." *Good grief! Seven hundred fifty dollars is cheap, sex-subsidized rent?! I'm so screwed!* Heather scrolled through the creepy search results and wondered why there were so many postings for sexy maid roommates. And whether people actually responded to the ads.

Then Heather found a listing that didn't sound sketchy: "$1,100 per month in a safe building for women. Make new friends!" She clicked on the link. The building was called The Zonderling, and it was in SoDeDyFa. She didn't know much about New York, but she'd definitely heard of the SoDeDyFa neighborhood because all the celebrities were photographed there. The Zonderling was the least creepy thing she'd found, and the rent included all utilities. Heather had enough money saved for a couple of months that would tide her over until she found a steady temp gig or job.

Heather's phone rang. It was her mom. *Ugh, not now.* Her phone then beeped with a text from her mom. Heather looked at it. "CHRISTINA'S MOM! HE IN ARGENTINA! WITH SUSIE BOYFRIEND! SHARE ARE YOU?????? DATELINE!!!!"

Heather texted back, "It's fine. I found a place."

Then she opened her map app on her phone. As she typed the address of The Zonderling, she noticed Larry's reflection in the mirror on the other side of the lobby. He was pulling a sexy Katniss costume from his closet and boxing it up with the bows and arrows.

What on earth? Christina! Heather was starting to think that she dodged a bullet by losing an apartment managed by Katniss-costume-loving Larry.

Heather stood on the curb in SoDeDyFa and stared at a sign above the door of a huge brownstone. She emptied a packet of cheese curds into her mouth as she reread the large bronze sign: "The Zonderling Hotel for Working Girls. Est. 1905 by the Altruistic Army." *Working girls?! Oh my God. Cleaning for Larry doesn't seem so bad anymore.*

The deep breath that Heather took to steady her nerves wasn't as rejuvenating as she had hoped. She nearly choked on the cheese curds as she inhaled the rotting garbage smell of August in New York City.

Welcome to New York! Heather thought as she climbed the steps of The Zonderling.

Two

Commander Vincent Van Der Linden founded the New York–based Altruistic Army in 1885. As a descendant of the Dutch settlers of New Amsterdam (i.e. the original New York, New York), Commander Van Der Linden was a visionary leader with a whole lot of fanciful ideas. Inspiration struck when he noticed a need for an evangelical group to promote, "singing more songs on street corners" and "fraternal brotherhood without libations." It was also very important to Commander Van Der Linden that all members wore military uniforms to show their commitment to bringing joy to nineteenth-century Manhattan.

On a sweltering August day, Vincent Van Der Linden gathered his family, friends, and attendees from a local temperance meeting. He created the Armed Forces of the Altruistic Singers—Altruistic Army for short—and gave himself the military title of *Commander*.

The turn-of-the-century street singing was met with hostility, especially when members allegedly spooked a bunch of carriage horses. The Altruistic Army denied any involvement in the Thanksgiving Horse Stampede of 1897, during which thirty horses destroyed the original headquarters of a fraternal organization known for its drinking, the Chivalrous Order of the Benevolent Lambda Lambs. This denial was in spite of a grainy photograph of Commander Van Der Linden's son-in-law, Charlie Van Der Zonderling, throwing branches at a large group of horses. The scared animals knocked over several kerosene lamps that subsequently torched the Benevolent Lambda Lambs. The district attorney didn't file charges because he was dating the other daughter of Commander Van Der Linden, and he didn't want to screw up a good thing with a chick who regularly put out.

Soon after the Benevolent Lambda Lambs incident, Commander Van Der Linden appointed his son-in-law to the position of *General*. As part of his new duties, General Charlie Van Der Zonderling was in charge of saving the vulnerable and impressionable young career girls who were moving to the city for work after the subway opened in 1904. Initial attempts to relocate the women back to their hometowns was so embarrassingly unsuccessful that Commander Van Der Linden reassigned General Van Der Zonderling to a soup kitchen in the run-down Der Linden district of old New Amsterdam.

One afternoon, while ladling his seventy-ninth bowl of chowder, General Van Der Zonderling was struck with the idea of a soup kitchen exclusively for young working girls—a soup kitchen where they could also sleep, learn Altruistic Army songs, and be safe from the likes of the Benevolent Lambda Lambs.

His dream came true in 1905 when The Zonderling Hotel for Working Girls opened its doors at 5678 New Holland Circle in the Der Linden district. The New Holland Circle address confused many New Yorkers because there were no circular streets to be found anywhere in the city. With such a misnomer, it was one of the hardest streets to find, which meant that it protected the residents twice as much. General Van Der Zonderling patted himself on the back for thinking of everything.

In order to make sure that these girls fell into no disrepute during their time in the big bad city, General Van Der Zonderling ordered all residents to take on-site classes in dancing, painting, and music. When he realized that most of the girls wanted to be in the theater, he added drama classes despite his great reservations against such a career choice that put women into close proximity to men at all hours of the day—and included kissing as public performance!

Over the years the number of classes dwindled, but out-of-state dreamers still flooded into The Zonderling like tourists swarmed Macy's at Christmas. These young women wanted to move to New York for new internships, new jobs, or a new start. But reality dealt a crushing blow when they learned that apartment rent was completely unaffordable unless they had a grandma with a rent-controlled apartment, which no one had because this grandma only existed in TV shows and movies. Monthly rent on a tiny New York studio usually equaled the monthly mortgage payment on a McMansion back home. Enter The Zonderling and its affordable rooms, meals, and security.

The Zonderling was an eccentric piece of old New York that somehow managed to survive into twenty-first-century America. If Realtors had their way, it wouldn't exist. They constantly made offers to turn the twenty-story building of four hundred units into a twenty-story building of nineteen units. But much to the Realtors' horror and astonishment, the Altruistic Army refused to sell. Selling the valuable SoDeDyFa building for over $150 million was inconceivable because it was against everything for which the Altruistic Army stood. No Altruistic Army member wanted to see The Zonderling gutted and turned into apartments for spoiled rich kids, a hideout for the mistresses of billionaires, or a tax haven for owners of dodgy foreign shell companies—basically the only three groups of people for whom new apartments were built nowadays in New York City.

There's nothing New York real estate agents loved more than a foreign billionaire, which is why they had worked hard to make the Der Linden into the high-end SoDeDyFa. For years the Der Linden had been synonymous with the decay of the 1970s and 1980s. It was so associated with urban blight that the city once referred to New Holland Circle as "the block of misery."

The misery took a turn for the worse in the late 1980s when a high-fashion designer opened a denim dye factory for its luxury 100%NYC line of blue jeans. Each pair of locally made jeans retailed for more than most people made in their weekly paychecks, but that "Made in NYC" tag was worth every penny to the wealthy customers who had probably never counted pennies in their lives. Despite the sliver of glamour that the designer brought to the area, the formaldehyde in the denim dye made the Der Linden smell like a high school biology lab on fetal pig dissection day. No one who could afford 100%NYC jeans lived within smelling range of the Der Linden. People nicknamed the area Der Smellen, and it became a go-to punch line for local stand-up comics. But ultimately nothing—formaldehyde stench be damned—stopped gentrification and the promise of sweet real estate commission.

Around 2005, shrewd real estate agents took a cue from the trendy TriBeCa (Triangle Below Canal) neighborhood and devised the name *SoDeDyFa* (South of the Denim Dye Factory) in order to draw people to the area in spite of the odor from a strong wind. The rebranding of Der Linden into SoDeDyFa worked extremely well with people who had never been to Der Smellen. Foreigners who missed out on TriBeCa real estate snapped up new apartments so they could have a pied-à-terre in a classic "rough" area of old New York. Within seven months of SoDeDyFa's invention, the neighborhood became one of the most expensive areas of Manhattan, bio-lab smell and all. The fact that the pungent odor came from the manufacture of luxury clothing made it an acceptable neighborhood idiosyncrasy—for about three more weeks.

After fielding dozens of influential calls from the wealthy SoDeDyFa residents, the owner of 100%NYC immediately moved the denim dye factory to an area of the city that would take at least twenty more years to gentrify. Local residents near the relocated factory weren't thrilled with the new funeral home smell in their neighborhood. Unfortunately they didn't know of anyone with enough clout to change anything because none of them had a cell phone number for anyone more influential than the middle school vice principal.

The billionaire real estate market had destroyed most of the old boardinghouses in New York. The Barbizon on the Upper East Side had gone condo years ago even though it was arguably the most iconic and famous hotel for women in the city. Former Barbizon residents included twentieth-century icons like Grace Kelly, Candice Bergen, Sylvia Plath, and Cloris Leachman. Even Don Draper dated a Barbizon girl on *Mad Men*, something that was bound to happen given the rate at which he went through glamorous women.

In the world of New York boardinghouses, the Barbizon was an elegant, fashionable sorority house. The Zonderling was a scrappy Muppets' Happiness Hotel.

THREE

Heather stood in The Zonderling's lobby, overwhelmed by the barrage of sounds assailing her. Someone, sight unseen, was playing the piano beautifully, but unfortunately there was a terrible voice singing along loudly and enthusiastically. It seemed like a song from *Aladdin* or *The Little Mermaid* but the voice was so bad that Heather couldn't decide. A crotchety old Russian lady, equally loud and enthusiastic, screamed into a phone as she sat inside one of several ancient wooden phone booths.

Suddenly a fierce-looking woman in her eighties slammed into Heather. The woman was carrying a walker but certainly didn't need to use it. Without breaking her stride, she turned around and hissed, "You didn't see *anything*." Then she trudged past a huge bulletin board and disappeared around a corner.

Seconds later she reappeared, walked to the bulletin board, ripped off a note about a missing TV remote, and vanished again. Plenty of notes remained on the bulletin board and ranged from fun activities (Movie Night now with popcorn!) to events (Annual Floradora Flip Social!) to the extremely bizarre (Keep treadmill clear of dumbwaiter!). Heather headed to the reception desk where a man was helping a bubbly brunette with her new room keys. The girl was in her early twenties and wore a North Dakota College T-shirt. The man was in his late fifties and wore a bright-red military uniform. He looked like a cross between a Canadian Mountie and a guard at Buckingham Palace, minus the silly hat. The green and gold *aiguillettes* hanging across his chest made him look like a Christmas nutcracker in training.

"Excuse me," Heather said.

The nutcracker gave her a huge smile. With a booming voice he said, "Well, hello, young lady! Welcome to The Zonderling! I'm The General, and this other young lady is Emily!"

"Hey!" said the North Dakota girl.

"I'm Heather Baumhauer. I called about a room."

"I'm moving in too!" Emily said.

"Yes! Welcome, Heather!" The General said. His head sharply turned as a twentysomething guy breezed past him. "Whoa! Young man! Young man!"

The guy stopped and lifted the headphones from one ear. "What?"

"What do you think you're doing? Who are you here to see?"

"Jennifer."

"Well that could be anybody. Who exactly—"

"Jennifer *Vang*."

"Very well," The General said as he opened a large, thick book with yellowed pages. "Sign in, and you can meet her in the parlor."

"Yeah, yeah. In the parlor. I know." The guy grabbed the pen and scribbled his name as quickly as he could.

"Thank you, son."

"This is so stupid," the man said under his breath as he put the headphones back over his ears and walked to the parlor.

"Now where was I?" The General turned back to Heather and Emily. "A room for Heather! You got here in the nick of time to grab one. Barbra just passed away. Let me get the form—"

"Wait, sorry. I'm getting a dead lady's room? Did she die in the room? Like *in* the room?"

"No, no. She died in the conservatory. Fell into the ficus after a heart attack."

"Good! Oh, I don't mean good that she's dead," Heather said, babbling and turning red-faced. "I'm sure she had many productive years ahead of her doing puzzles, living independently, watering plants, cutting coupons. Just following up—how did she die in the conservatory?" Heather immediately began fighting a smile, and joked, "Mrs. Peacock with the wrench?"

A look of panic washed over The General's face as he asked, "Did you see a wrench?"

"Um, no."

The General's face softened in relief. "Thank goodness! I thought Loretta found one. We had to hide them after the Flag Day talent show."

The General told Emily and Heather about the annual talent revue that took place a few weeks ago. Everything had been going smoothly, and the cafetorium was beautifully decorated in American flags. So many flags that The General actually wondered for a moment whether there was too much bunting. Then he laughed at the thought. *Too much bunting! There can never be enough bunting!*

As he chuckled to himself in the front row of seats, a cute Southern girl named Lauren marched onstage. She was holding a baton and wearing a dress sewn from American flags. Lauren centered herself, nodded to the lady at the piano, and began singing and twirling the baton.

"Yankee Doodle went to town, ridin'—"

Clunk! A wrench flew out of the audience and knocked Lauren to the ground. Her baton spun out of her hand and struck the piano lady. As soon as Lauren hit the floor, Loretta's voice yelled from the audience, "You're no Yankee!"

The General thought hard about the right word to use to describe Loretta to Emily and Heather. "*Passionate*. Loretta's very passionate about Flag Day. And America. And channel surfing."

"She can't miss her stories, eh?" Emily said.

"Definitely not! That's why she was arguing with Barbra. The kerfuffle started in the parlor, also known as the TV room, next to the conservatory. It was during Loretta's favorite show, *Beauty Queen Dial-Up*."

Beauty Queen Dial-Up was a new hit reality show on broadcast television that had been number one all summer. It was so huge that it easily won its time slot on a consistent basis, helped by its popular lead-in, *Win a Sugar Daddy*. Naturally there were already thirty-two knockoffs in development at rival networks. The premise for *Beauty Queen Dial-Up* was that five teenage beauty queens had to live together in one house in the middle of Nebraska with no Wi-Fi and no cell phones. Their only contact with the outside world was one dial-up modem. Miss Beauty Queen Vermont, Miss Beauty Queen Delaware, Miss Beauty Queen Oregon, Miss Beauty Queen Alabama, and Miss Beauty Queen Idaho were having a tough time dealing with the heavy analog books as their only entertainment. Miss Beauty Queen Delaware was currently in the middle of a breakdown—she kept hearing phantom text alerts and recently went all *Tell-Tale Heart*, ripping up several floorboards in search of the noise. All age groups agreed that it was riveting television.

"After Barbra passed we immediately started a no-channel-surfing policy," The General said. "It's early days though."

Suddenly a blaring fire alarm screeched to life.

"Oyster crackers!" The General exclaimed. "When will those French girls learn that they can't smoke inside?" He grabbed a French dictionary. "I'll be right back for orientation in my office."

The General hurried away, leaving the two women alone at the desk. The Russian lady was unflustered by the noise and continued yelling into the phone in Russian about how Americans couldn't cook a proper beef stroganoff.

A nineteen-year-old resident poked her head around the corner. She looked at Heather and Emily and asked in a French accent, "Zee General?"

"He just left," Heather said.

The French girl nodded and said, "Good." She ran to the main door, opened it, and pulled a guy inside. "*Dépêche toi! Allons-y!*" she barked in French as she dragged him through the lobby and around the corner.

Emily and Heather looked at each other. *What was that about?* The blaring fire alarm noise stopped a few seconds later and was replaced by the horrible singing of random Disney songs. Emily giggled.

"I don't know which is worse," she laughed.

"She's so, so bad, right?" Heather said.

"I don't know," Emily replied. She gestured to the Russian lady. "She seems to like it." Then Emily switched to a Russian accent and said, "Music make me happy, like little girl mining for coal in Siberia."

"Your accent is great! Are you an actress?" Heather asked.

"I am! Thanks so much! I brushed up on my Russian while watching *Air Force One* on the plane ride here."

Emily had indeed watched the Harrison Ford movie and worked on her accent while on the plane to New York. She was so engrossed that she failed to notice the two passengers next to her had abandoned their middle and aisle seats. Sitting alone by the window, she repeatedly practiced her Russian by saying, "Maybe there is bomb, Mr. President. I hijacking plane!"

As she said the line a third time, she heard a stern female voice yell, "*Freeze!*"

Emily screamed and put her hands in the air when she saw a federal air marshal pointing a gun at her. A rowdy mob of passengers filled the aisle, armed with the contents of carry-on luggage, including a saxophone, a box of pralines, duty-free perfume, a cricket bat, mini vodka bottles, and a Hawaiian pineapple.

"My flight from North Dakota included a pretty long emergency landing in Detroit," Emily acknowledged.

Every new Zonderling resident had to sit through orientation with The General. Many women spent a lot of time staring at the huge black-and-white photograph of General Van Der Zonderling that hung on the wall. Most people said that he looked deranged. The General said that he looked passionate.

In the photograph, General Van Der Zonderling wore a uniform similar to the one worn by The General. The most distinguishing part of General Van Der Zonderling's appearance was the huge handlebar mustache with a shaved one-inch section underneath his nose. He adopted it after seeing a European prince with a similar style, and so it made him feel classy and important. However, General Van Der Zonderling didn't realize that the reason the prince's mustache was missing the one-inch section was because he got too close to a birthday candle.

The photo also depicted General Van Der Zonderling wearing his signature two monocles. He preferred them to traditional glasses because he thought monocles made him look more like a member of high society. But monocles were difficult to keep in both eyes at the same time, and they constantly popped off his face when he raised his eyebrows. This had been most problematic when he greeted new people at the soup kitchen.

Heather kept staring at the unsettling image. General Van Der Zonderling's wild eyes followed her as she tried to concentrate on what The General was saying.

"Another actress! That's just fabulous, Emily!" The General said. "Did you know that Kristen Johnston used to live here?"

"Wow! So neat!" Emily said. "Who's that?"

"Who's that? Sally Solomon from *3rd Rock from the Sun*, that's who! Her name's in the guest book," The General proudly said. "Well, at least we think so. But how many K. Johnstons could there be?"

"This place really is just like that Katharine Hepburn movie! You know, the one about a boardinghouse for actresses in New York."

"Except unlike the movie *Stage Door*, there's never been a successful suicide in our great history here at The Zonderling," The General said.

"Wait," Heather said. "What's the number of unsuccessful—nope, forget it. I don't want to know."

The General didn't notice her question anyway because he was about to tell the greatest story ever told.

"It's the greatest story ever told!" The General said. "This glorious building was established in 1905 by General Charlie Van Der Zonderling, the son-in-law of the founder of the Altruistic Army himself!" The General saluted the photo of General Van Der Zonderling. "The new subway started bringing young ladies into this city of sin by the hundreds. To make sure they didn't cut their hair or start wearing pants, he opened this haven for the city's working girls. The Melanie Griffith kind, of course."

Whew, Heather thought.

"I was transferred here several years ago upon my promotion to General. I started my early Army career chopping carrots at the Der Linden Soup Kitchen."

"I love soup! And carrots!" Emily said.

"Me too! Sometimes, I prefer stew if—"

Heather interrupted. She didn't want to go off track again, like when Emily and The General spent five minutes talking about how to keep fountain pens from leaking on airplanes. "If we could backtrack to the guidelines that you were explaining earlier—"

"Absolutely no more than two eggs per person at breakfast. Not after the brunch bedlam of 2010," The General said.

"No, not about eggs. I got that loud and clear from your overhead presentation. I'm referring to the rule about no men in the building."

"I think you misheard me."

"I thought so," Heather laughed. "I was like, no men in the building? What is this? A nunnery?"

"No, no!" The General shook his head. "The nunnery is *downtown*. At The Zonderling, gentlemen are allowed in the parlor after they've been checked in at reception."

Whaaaaaat?

"And I'm hip enough to know all the tricks for sneaking them into your room with fancy wigs and high heels," The General said. "I've seen Tom Hanks in *Bosom Buddies*."

FOUR

Heather and Emily dragged their luggage across the lobby and toward the elevator. They nearly knocked over a food cart that an Altruistic Army member was pushing toward the cafetorium for dinner. Heather was in a daze as she thought about the bizarre rules rattled off by her new nutcracker landlord. If she had carefully read The Zonderling's website while sitting in Larry's lobby, she wouldn't have been surprised by the building's Altruistic Army origin and no-men policy. Though to be fair, Heather hadn't even been quite sure what a *boardinghouse* was to begin with, other than she could afford it and it was located in a trendy neighborhood that she read about on Twitter.

All things considered, The Zonderling was pretty much on par with the nonstop apartment-related sacrifices that New Yorkers made to live in the city that never sleeps. No one justified ridiculous apartments as frequently as New Yorkers. The common rationale of residents at The

Zonderling was something like, "I have to share a bathroom with strangers and my boyfriend can never come over, but it's an awesome location." It was really no weirder than the way other New Yorkers rationalized their apartments that they could barely afford: "It's a twelfth-floor walk-up railroad apartment, but it's only three blocks from the subway" or "My knees touch the bathroom wall when I sit on the toilet, but at least the kitchen is big enough for an oven" or "I think the guy down the hall owns a pet tiger, but I haven't seen a rat in five weeks." In spite of the no-men and no-alcohol policies, most New Yorkers, upon learning of The Zonderling, agreed that $1,100 per month for a room in SoDeDyFa was a steal. *That includes breakfast, dinner, and utilities? Where do I sign up? I'll be Peter Scolari. I don't care!*

"You can do this. It's just like a dorm," Heather mumbled to herself.

"Only it's the best dorm ever!" Emily squealed. "There's, like, three signs that say *fallout shelter*. There are real phone booths with doors. And there's a dumbwaiter straight out of an Agatha Christie book! We're living in an old-timey movie, Heather!" Emily stopped to read the dinner menu posted by the cafetorium. "I'm starving. Want dinner?"

"No, I'm going to take my bags to my room," Heather said as she pushed the elevator button.

"Oh for cute!" Emily said as she read the menu. "Beef wrapped in pastry! Called a Wellington! That's so fancy. Jeez, I can't wait to meet the sophisticated New Yorkers who live here!" Emily waved good-bye and pushed her luggage into the cafetorium to make new friends.

The elevator doors opened a few seconds later, revealing a middle-aged woman with dirty glasses and long stringy hair. Heather quietly got in and pressed the button for the twelfth floor. She could feel the woman's eyes on her.

"Hi," the woman said, speaking only on long, slow, exhale breaths. "Are you new?"

"Yep."

"That's a pretty shirt."

"Thanks." Heather willed the elevator to move faster. The old lady gave her the heebie-jeebies just like her college history professor who always looked down her shirt.

The woman noticed the room number on Heather's key. "Room 1216. How nice. You're in Barbra's room," she breathed. "A new young neighbor. About time. I'm next door."

The elevator stopped on the twelfth floor. *Finally!* The doors opened and Heather scooted into the hall. The weird lady followed, loudly shuffling her feet across the carpet as if she lacked the energy to lift them. Heather found her room and tried to shove her luggage inside as fast as she could.

"Need some help?"

"I've got it. Thanks." Heather quickly shut the door and stumbled inside.

Her phone beeped with a text from her mom: "Call me so I knit you're Alice!!!"

Better get this over with. Heather called her parents' landline. Her dad picked up, and he gave her an update on her AWOL cousin.

"Supposedly," Jim said, "Christina met some Australian who was traveling on an around-the-world airplane ticket. He convinced her to go with him."

"She left me alone in New York to go on a trip with a random guy?"

"Well, apparently he looks like the Australian Channing Tatum."

"Still," Heather said, even though she might have done the same thing.

"So where are you?"

"I found a place in SoDeDyFa."

"Soda what?"

"It's kind of like a dorm for adults."

Heather could hear her mom talking in the background. Sally loudly asked, "Is that Heather? Give me the phone!"

"Dad, I don't have time for Mom. Just tell her everything's fine."

"Will do! Bye!"

Before her dad hung up, Heather heard her mom yell, "Jim! Did you tell her to stay out of Times Square? It's full of crack cocaine!"

Heather put her phone in her pocket and looked around the 110-square-foot old-fashioned room. It was a space that would have been called a walk-in closet if it had it been in her parents' house. It seemed even smaller than her college dorm room, but at least there was a large window that faced a quiet residential street. The desk, bed, dresser, and nightstand reminded her of stackable dorm furniture. The closet was a freestanding wardrobe that looked older than her grandma. The inside was covered in political stickers that confirmed its age and Barbra's obsession with politicians running on Y2K scare tactics ("Turn back to paper in 2000, not the year 1900! Desuet for Congress").

Little did Heather know that some of the most famous residents of The Zonderling had used the same furniture in Room 1216: Edith Spauldenhead, British World War II journalist; Stefani Washington, former painter and current Silicon Valley billionaire; and most famous of all, failed actress Cindy Mickleton. Cindy was mostly known for a 1996 affair that brought down a Kentucky congressman who was running on a platform of restoring family values. Cindy went on to a very successful career as owner of the most popular manicure salon in southeast Kansas, entirely financed from her tell-all royalties.

Much like the illustrious residents before her, Heather sweated buckets as she stood inside Room 1216. Only a handful of shared space was air-conditioned, on account of the ancient electrical situation, which made summer a long, sweaty slog. Heather immediately opened the window. She looked up at the transom above the door, but it was painted shut. Luckily, there was a ceiling fan. Heather turned it on, and a cloud of disgusting dust immediately rained down upon her. Apparently Barbra liked sitting in a hot room of dead air.

Heather grabbed her keys and headed to the shared bathroom to rinse off her dust-covered face. She hesitated entering when she heard angry voices inside.

"No way! Stop it!" a young female voice yelled.

A familiar voice said, "You can't tell me what to do."

"And you can't make up your own rules just because you've been here since the Nixon administration!"

"I can use a clothesline if I want to."

"No one wants to see your underwear, Loretta!"

The infamous Loretta! Heather was anxious to finally see the face of the wrench-throwing, reality TV–loving weirdo.

"Well, there's nothing you can do about it," Loretta taunted.

"If you keep hanging up your underwear, it's all going in the garbage as soon as you leave."

"You can't do that!"

"Watch me! I'll untie the whole line and toss it in the trash."

"Then I'll stay here until they're all dry. You can't make me leave."

The other voice snorted with derision. "Doesn't *Beauty Queen Dial-Up* start soon?"

"Crap!"

"Get this all out of here. Now!"

Loretta exited the bathroom with an armful of underwear and smashed into Heather. It was the same lady with the walker in the lobby. Loretta immediately recognized Heather and viciously whispered, "You saw *nothing!*"

"Excuse me?"

"Nothing!"

"OK."

Satisfied, Loretta skulked down the hallway carrying a week's worth of frayed underwear attached to a clothesline. As she neared the corner, Loretta ran into the French girl and the boyfriend she'd smuggled inside. "What do you think you're doing?"

The French girl looked at her boyfriend. "She's the crazy one I told you about!" she said in English to make sure that Loretta understood.

"Ah, *oui*," he said. "The sticks!"

"*Oui.*"

"Speak American in America!" Loretta yelled. "I'm calling The General immediately!"

"OK, Loretta. We leave. *Allons-y*," the French girl said as she led her boyfriend into the stairwell.

"Out!" Loretta yelled. "Have some respect! You'd be speaking German if it weren't for us!"

As the stairwell door closed, Heather thought she heard a curse word that she learned in French class, but she wasn't certain. Loretta sure didn't care because she had already disappeared into her room with her underwear.

Heather continued into the bathroom, which also reminded her of her old dorm with the multiple sinks, toilets, and shower stalls. The Zonderling was starting to feel like an alternate timeline where people lived forever in college dorms. Several signs, ranging in temperament, were taped to the wall. One was typed on Altruistic Army letterhead and read: "Do not blow dry your hair in your room! Only use hair dryers in the bathroom!" There were also other handwritten signs such as: "Your mom doesn't live here. Clean up your freaking mess! You are disgusting!" and "Really?! Flush the damn toilet!" Someone had crossed off the word *damn* and wrote *language* above it.

As she made her way inside, Heather spotted the source of the young female voice. It was a woman in her late twenties who was wearing pajamas and brushing her teeth. Her long black hair was tied back in a quick ponytail, but the dark violet highlights were still visible in the fluorescent light. She looked like she was getting ready for bed even though it was dinnertime.

The woman noticed Heather. "Sorry for yelling, but Loretta is the worst," she said. "And when I say the worst, I mean she'll flush the toilets when you're in the shower. The only safe time to shower is during her post-afternoon-talk-show nap."

"Good to know," Heather said quietly. She turned on the faucet at one of the sinks and splashed water on her face. She eyed the woman's pajamas in the mirror.

Noticing Heather's stare, the woman said, "Oh, yeah, the pajamas. I start work at two a.m."

"Yikes! What do you do?"

"Trade support, equity. I'm on the European markets, hence the early start time." The woman extended her hand to Heather. "Jennifer Vang."

Upon hearing the news of Jennifer's fancy-sounding job, Heather perked up. "That's why I moved here!" Heather said as she shook Jennifer's hand. "I want to do something like that! Or anything international, really. I have an interview tomorrow with a temp agency for a finance job. I'm so excited to finally be in New York, see Wall Street, and—"

"Aw, that's so cute. You remind me of my New York honeymoon period. Your enthusiasm is kind of nice to see." Jennifer sighed. "But pretty soon you'll ruin your nice dress because you sat in muddy boot prints on the subway. Or mayonnaise. Or water, and then realize it's definitely *not* water."

"How often does that happen?"

"Every time it rains."

"I mean the mayonnaise."

"Once a month?" Jennifer shrugged. "People eat a lot of stuff on the train. It all makes you want to go somewhere normal where you'd actually be surprised if you sat in mayonnaise."

Heather said jokingly, "At least I'd get away from the creepy lady in the room next to me."

"Which one?"

There's more than one?

"Does she have insane hair like she stands outside during storms and yells at pigeons in Portuguese? Or does she constantly hum like a refrigerator? Or," Jennifer said, imitating the voice of Heather's neighbor, "does she only talk like this, on exhale breaths, and shuffle her feet? Or—"

"She talks like that."

"That's Benjamin Button."

"Like the Brad Pitt movie? Why do you call her that?"

"Because she looks like she's fifty."

"How old is she?"

"Twenty-six."

"She's only *twenty-six?*"

"Four years at The Zonderling have been rough on her."

"Jeez. She looks like she could be my mom."

"You should also be on the lookout for Stinky Carrie and Porn Lisa, not to be confused with Normal Lisa. Normal Lisa is cool."

"What's the deal with the lady who was just in here?"

"The lovely lady you just met is Loretta, and Helen is her best friend. I'm sure you'll run into Helen soon because all she ever does is hang around in here complaining about something stupid, like the new paint is too bright, or the toilet paper is the wrong ply. Of course she's not bothered by whatever Loretta does with all that crap in that shower."

Jennifer pointed to a shower, and Heather peeked inside. There was a box of baking soda, an empty clothesline, a Farmers' Almanac from 2007, an unused grass-scented candle, a pile of paper towels, an aerosol spray can, and a mason jar full of frayed tree sticks.

"What are the sticks for?"

"I thought about asking. But then I realized there's no possible answer that I'd be OK with hearing."

"How do you live here?"

Earnestly, Jennifer said, "Location! It's an amazing—" She cut herself off as she noticed something out the window. She bent down, put her face against the screen, and yelled, "Hey! Do not walk away from the dog poop! Yeah, I see you. This whole city is *Rear Window*! Pick it up, jackass!"

Oh, man, this woman is bananas too. "Thanks for the advice and warnings, Jennifer." Heather began backing up out of the bathroom.

Jennifer stood up from the window and had dark soot on her nose and forehead from the screen. "One last thing. Always have emergency tissues in your pocket. The toilet paper has been disappearing fast recently. I was stuck in here for five minutes yesterday until Normal Lisa rescued me."

"Right. Well, thanks, Jennifer! I gotta go. I have to get out. *Up!* I mean get up early. For work. Big temp interview tomorrow!"

"Good luck!" Jennifer said. Then she caught the reflection of her soot-covered face in the mirror. *Of course.* Jennifer sighed. *I hate New York.*

Heather was in Barbra's old twin bed and trying to fall asleep. It was not going well. She looked at her phone. Christina hadn't answered any of her texts. Heather couldn't believe that her cousin had been so flaky and irresponsible.

Then Heather remembered that when Christina moved to Manhattan, she arrived at the airport two hours late and missed her flight because she kept redoing her makeup. But then Christina realized that she had shown up a week before Flight 608, on which she was actually booked, so she ended up leaving on time for New York after all. Only Christina would show up two hours late but one week early.

Heather's mind raced with a million thoughts as she grappled with the new reality of living in New York. Living in a boardinghouse of weirdos. Living in a dead woman's room.

"Everything's fine," she said to herself. "You'll fall asleep and wake up in New York, and everything is going to be fine."

"And I'm here if you need anything," Benjamin Button said through the wall.

Heather quickly pulled the sheets over her head. *And living in a future episode of* Dateline.

FIVE

"What are you doing?" an old voice yelled from inside the bathroom. "What exactly are you doing with that soap?"

Wearing a robe, Heather paused by the bathroom door, struggling to hold onto her hair dryer and multiple bottles of shampoo, conditioner, and soap. She needed to get into the bathroom to shower before her temp interview, but she didn't want to get involved in whatever was happening inside. Again. The bathrooms were the hub of all activity at The Zonderling because it was the one place that every resident had to use no matter what. Well, nearly every resident.

Several months ago, Normal Lisa went into the bathroom to fill a water bottle and swore that she saw Loretta pouring soup cans of yellow liquid down the sink drain. When confronted, Loretta said it was no one's business what she poured into the sink so long as it wasn't vegetable soup. "Martha's the one who clogs the drains with chunky soup!"

Loretta yelled, changing the subject. From that day forward, Normal Lisa only drank purchased bottled water. Similar rumors about Loretta peeing into cans in her room were sporadic, unconfirmed, and seemed tied to airdates of reality show season finales.

"Excuse me?" asked a voice that sounded like Emily.

"What do you mean?"

"You can't do that in the sink!" the old voice yelled. "No way."

An old woman barged out of the bathroom. She unapologetically bumped into Heather, dislodging a bottle of shampoo from her arms, and marched down the hall without acknowledging her actions. Heather bent down to pick up the bottle and noticed black oxford shoes in front of her as she kneeled down.

"You need a shower caddy," the woman said.

Heather looked up, and as her eyes traveled from the oxford shoes to the woman's face (via a conservative business dress), she was surprised to find a pretty twentysomething staring back at her instead of a middle-aged schoolteacher.

"I got one at the shop around the corner," the oxford-shoe girl said.

"Thanks for the tip. I need to remember to buy one today."

"I'm guessing that you just moved in. I'm Lisa. Welcome to the twelfth floor!"

"Nice to meet you. I'm Heather."

"Cool, well, I have to run to work, but you're welcome to come to movie night in my room tonight. Some girls and I are watching *Fifty Shades of Grey*."

"That's really nice of you, but I think I'll pass. Fingers crossed, I'll have a new job to start tomorrow—I don't want to be up late."

"No prob. We do our own movie night on the regular, so maybe next time. See ya!" Lisa waved good-bye.

Heather walked into the bathroom and saw Emily brushing her teeth.

"Morning, Emily!"

"Hi, um...oh no. Don't tell me your name! I know I know it." Emily scrunched up her face as she racked her brain. "You're from Wisconsin...where Milwaukee is...where people make beer...that gives people hangovers...which is a movie with Heather Graham! Good morning, *Heather*!"

"That was quite a journey."

"It's called a mnemonic device. I learned about it in drama club."

"But to get started, how did you remember that I'm from Wisconsin?"

"I don't know." Emily went back to brushing her teeth. "Oh shoot! I could have gotten there faster. Milwaukee straight to Heather Graham since she was born there!"

"I'm terrible with names too. I don't even remember who I just met in the hall."

"That girl who was in here? Her name is Lisa. I heard her invite you too," Emily said with a mouthful of toothpaste.

"To watch *Fifty Shades?*"

"That she watches all the time. It's apparently all she ever shows at her movie night." Emily took the toothbrush out of her mouth and whispered, "I think that's Porn Lisa, not Normal Lisa."

Heather peeked into a shower stall. It looked clean, unlike the one where Loretta stored her jar of sticks.

"What are you doing today?" Emily asked. "I'm going to visit all of the places from my favorite movies and TV shows. You're welcome to come along."

"I have an interview with a temp agency. I gotta shower and get ready."

"Awesome! Good luck!" Emily gave her a thumbs-up and began flossing.

"Thanks," Heather said as she closed the shower stall door.

She turned on the water and turned the knob toward *hot*. The closer she got toward *hot*, the colder it seemed to get. After a freezing moment of shivering, she turned the knob back toward *cold*, and the water got warmer. Moments after figuring out that the shower knob was on backward, Heather heard several footsteps enter the bathroom.

"There she is!" said the voice of the same old lady who'd knocked the shampoo out of Heather's arms. "Look at what she's doing, Loretta!"

"Exactly what are you doing with that soap and towel?" Loretta asked.

"I washed my face," Emily said.

"Oh, really?" Loretta sneered.

"Look at that mess she made!" the other old lady said.

"From washing my face," Emily answered. "I can wipe up the water around the sink."

There was a long silence, and Heather tried to figure out what was going on.

"I guess the evidence supports your claim," Loretta said. "Helen here thought you were taking a bath in the sink."

"Like a sponge bath?" Emily said.

"It happens," Helen said. "Sometimes you just don't want to bother with a full—"

"Even if you were just washing your face, don't make a mess," Loretta said.

"Exactly! That's how eye infections spread," Helen added.

"And mold. Black mold!" Loretta said. "Do you know how dangerous *black mold* is?"

"It won't be a problem because I definitely won't be bathing in the sink," Emily said.

"You millennials have no concept of cleanliness," Loretta said.

"Look, I'm cleaning it up right now!" Emily said. "You know, I don't think we've met. I'm Emily. I just moved in."

"Figures you're new. I'm Loretta. This is Helen."

"Have you been here long?" Emily asked.

"What kind of question is that?"

"Just a friendly one. An ice breaker as they say back home."

"Which is where?"

Undeterred, Emily continued in vain to make a friend. "Whynot, North Dakota."

Loretta snorted with disdain. "No wonder you were washing your face."

"They let just anyone move in," Helen said. "I remember when—"

Loretta inhaled sharply. "*What* is that smell?"

"Smells like Fresh Italian Laundry," Emily said, correctly naming the scent of Heather's shampoo from national chain Body Scrubs and Other Things.

"*Disgusting!*" Loretta shouted in the direction of Heather's shower.

Heather ignored Loretta, pretending that she didn't hear her over the sound of the water.

"That smell is awful, Loretta!" Helen said. "I can barely breathe! I have to get out of here." Heather heard Helen stomp out of the bathroom.

"No stinky products allowed in here!" Loretta yelled to Heather. "Can't you read the note? Or can't you read anything that's not on your phone?"

"What note? I didn't see one about—" Emily asked, before she was drowned out by the sound of air freshener that Loretta removed from "her" shower stall. Or at least that's what Heather assumed when she heard someone spraying an aerosol can. Emily and Heather both coughed as a bleach-based product—that definitely wasn't air freshener—filled the air.

"That's mold cleaner!" Emily sputtered.

"You're welcome!" Loretta said. "As per usual, no one ever thanks me for all I do here to keep this place clean."

"You can't spray that like air freshener!" Emily said.

"So you want mold in here?"

"Of course not!"

"If you're going to make messes and leave garbage everywhere, maybe I should report you to The General for being filthy in the bathroom."

"I just got here! I haven't—"

"I suppose I can look the other way if you help me carry my garbage outside. You seem to be proficient in garbage."

"Sure," Emily said. "Just stop spraying that. It's awful!"

"It's disgusting that you want to live in such a mess." The spraying stopped. "Well, let's go! My garbage isn't going to carry itself outside."

Heather heard Emily and Loretta start to walk out of the bathroom. One set of footsteps stopped, and a toilet flushed.

"Showers longer than three minutes are why the Chinese are taking over, you air-conditioned pansies!" Loretta yelled. "Come on, North Dakota. Move it!" Two sets of footsteps exited the bathroom.

Luckily Heather had already rinsed her hair, so she could quickly hop out of the scalding hot shower. She put on her robe, exited the stall, and turned on the window fan for some fresh air. Still gagging on the smell of the mold cleaner, Heather plugged in her hair dryer.

Sweat poured down her face from the hot blow dryer and the stuffy warm bathroom. *This is worse than that family road trip when the AC broke in the Badlands.* She moved closer to the breeze from the window fan and bent over to dry her roots. The fan suddenly stopped blowing, and when Heather bolted upright to fix the problem, she was surprised to see Loretta staring at her.

"This fan has to be on *exhaust* so that the hot air is sucked out," Loretta said. "You were bringing in more hot air."

"Without AC it's all hot air no matter which way it goes," Heather said.

"Don't be stupid."

"The other setting creates air circulation that evaporates the sweat on your skin."

"No, it doesn't."

"Yes, that makes it feel cooler."

"No."

"But that's how fans work."

"No, it's not."

"Yes, it is. It's like the whole point of a fan."

"It has to be on exhaust."

"Well, I'm in here now and want it on normal until I'm done. I have a job interview—"

"I have seniority."

"I don't think you understand. That's not what—"

"It stays on exhaust," Loretta said. Then she pulled off the knob on the fan, put it in her pocket, and left the bathroom.

Six

Peter's Principle Staffing was a successful global temp agency based in Missouri. Founded by Peter Czarwowski, the company had grown like gangbusters since the 2008 recession. After the market collapse, corporations decided that benefit-free temporary employees looked way, way better at the bottom of their unwieldy, multicolored spreadsheets. Temps were also easier to fire because they weren't real *heads*, the useful HR word for describing employees. A person who was a nonhead (in spite of having an actual head) was super easy to get rid of compared to a real head. Peter's Principle Staffing was more than eager to help companies cut costs by adding lots of cheap benefit-free nonheads.

Temps also filled a need for a certain group of very, very busy full-time employees. These employees spent most of their days working hard to look busy (i.e. scheduling, prepping, and attending as many meetings as possible). They never actually did any work, but no one noticed because they looked so busy with all of their meetings. Since they had mastered the art of looking overwhelmed, it was easy for them to convince their bosses to hire temps. Once the temps arrived, these employees finally had the time they needed to attend all of their very important meetings about needing more meetings.

After a brief morning of half-assed training, many temps went unsupervised by their meeting-straddled incompetent managers. Other employees didn't pay attention to the nonheads either, because on principle, they never talked to temps. The only exception was if the temp was a cute girl, which then meant constant attention from all married men within a twenty-desk radius.

With such a complete lack of supervision, many temps never knew what they were supposed to be doing for eight hours a day. This was especially true for temps at large corporations, places where HR didn't fully understand what 47 percent of real heads were doing anyway due to job descriptions bursting with corporate jargon.

Peter's Principle Staffing was excellent at filling positions with convoluted job descriptions because they knew that there was a direct relationship between use of corporate jargon and ineptness of the hiring manager. As such, Peter's Principle Staffing was the most sought-after temp agency in New York City. Their Manhattan office was on the eighteenth floor of a shabby building sandwiched between a liquor shop and a discount luggage store named Luggage Things d/b/a Cameras! Gifts! Wallets!

When Heather entered the ground floor lobby, the security guard laughed at her Wisconsin ID and told her that she was crazy to ever have lived in such a cold place. Then unbeknownst to Heather, he took her photo. This awkward photo was then printed on a building pass that she had to wear in order to get past the turnstiles.

Once she got to the eighteenth floor, Heather knocked on the glass door of Peter's Principle Staffing. Their motto—*America's Cheapest Nonheads*—was etched into the glass.

The receptionist buzzed Heather inside without looking up from her computer. "What?" she demanded.

"I have an appointment to get a temp job. I'm Heather Baumhauer."

"I don't think so," the receptionist said. She was completely exasperated.

"Oh no. Don't tell me that I wrote it down wrong."

"Don't talk to me like that."

"I'm sorry. I thought it was—"

"Are you listening?"

"Yes."

"Because I'm only going to say this once."

"If you can just get me in today. I really need a job and—"

"Because I'm your mother!"

"What?"

"Now let your brother inside before I call Mr. O'Neill!"

The woman ripped a pair of ear buds, hidden under her long hair, from her ears and threw them on her desk as she ended her phone call. She looked up at Heather and asked, "You have kids?"

"No."

"Don't!"

"Sorry."

"Sorry? Why are you sorry? You didn't knock me up."

"Well, I just...you seem pretty stressed out."

"You would be too if your idiot son kept trapping his little brother on the damn fire escape."

"Probably," Heather said. "Um, I have an appointment?"

Tanya Gonzales was having an even worse day than the receptionist at Peter's Principle Staffing. Tanya had been asked to staff fifteen positions in obscure departments by tomorrow for her biggest client, International Bank. International Bank loved temps, and they loved Tanya for sending them temps. The company especially loved not paying for health insurance, vacation days, or sick days. Peter's Principle Staffing was the answer to all of the prayers from International Bank's accountants, stockholders, and lazy employees.

Tanya also heard that someone caught one of her temps making out with a junior vice president in the elevator. So that was another temp to replace by tomorrow. And now she had to deal with this earnest girl from Wisconsin who was sitting in front of her. Heather was working on Tanya's last nerve.

"Basically I want to work in something like Wall Street or advertising or at a consulate," Heather said. "Something just really international."

Tanya tried not to roll her eyes at the cluelessness. She looked at Heather's resume. "You have a master's in Scandinavian Studies. What on earth is that for?"

"I know some Swedish. Maybe I can translate at the UN."

"I don't think so."

"Knowing Swedish means that I can also understand Norwegian and Danish," Heather offered.

"No one is going to hire you as a translator. What are your computer scores?" Tanya flipped through the test results for the computer tests that Heather just completed. "You rated intermediate to advanced on all of the basic programs."

"Can I redo them? I didn't really understand how the test worked, and I know—"

"Redo them? Most people who come through here barely rate intermediate."

"The computer screen froze when I—"

"You can make a spreadsheet, you speak English, and you don't talk in Tweets. You're fine." Tanya punched a few keys on her computer. "I think I have a job for you. It starts tomorrow."

"Oh my gosh! Like the UN or something?"

"Similar," Tanya hedged. "It is international."

"That's so cool! What is it?"

Tanya looked at her computer screen and read the job title. "Administrative assistant in the NRI department at International Bank."

"What's the NRI?"

"No idea. Be there at nine in the morning. Ask for Vikram Singh."

Heather jotted down the address for International Bank and left Peter's Principle Staffing with a sense of accomplishment. She headed home to The Zonderling with a big smile on her face, even though some unidentifiable liquid dripped onto her from the ceiling of the subway station while she waited for the train.

SEVEN

The air hung hot, heavy, and smelly in The Zonderling hallway. The combination of no hallway windows and no air conditioning made the boardinghouse feel like being below deck on a ship. The Zonderling was like a self-sustained cruise ship afloat in New York—it had everything one needed for an adventure in the Big Apple. The intrepid and motivated took daytrips to the island of Manhattan. The fearful and narrow-minded never left the boat.

As Emily walked to her room on the twelfth floor of The SS Zonderling, she noticed an unusually cool breeze that felt good on her sweaty skin. Locating the cool breeze became her number one priority, even higher than finding the location of the *Friends* fountain in Central Park so she could take a selfie. This change in priorities was a smart move, considering that the *Friends* fountain was over two thousand miles away on the Warner Bros. Ranch in Burbank, California.

Emily immediately traced the cool breeze to two across-the-hall neighbors who had their doors and windows open. The open doors created a cross draft between the windows that cooled both rooms. This would not have astonished Emily had she paid more attention in physics class, but Josh Ferreira sat in front of her, and staring at his gorgeousness took up all of her time.

Emily propped her door open with her suitcase, then knocked on the door immediately across from hers to share the brilliant revelation about working together to create a draft. The door opened a crack. Loretta's face appeared in the dim light as she shouted into a cell phone, "It was *two* for five sheets this morning. Don't try to change it to five for five. Who do you take me for, Miss Beauty Queen Delaware? Hold on." She looked at Emily and barked, "What?"

"As you know—"

"I'm not going to have another garbage bag for you to carry out until tomorrow."

Emily tried to look into Loretta's room. She couldn't see much in the four inches of space between the door and the doorframe, except an open soup can with yellow liquid sitting on the dresser. She spotted a few floor-to-ceiling piles of stuff, including something that looked like wrenches, which worried Emily considerably.

"OK, but that's not why I'm here," Emily said. "It's really hot—"

"And?"

"I was just wondering if you would—"

"No."

"If you wanted to keep your door open—"

"No."

"We could get a draft going between our windows. The girls down the hall are doing it, and it's so much—"

"No." As Loretta closed the door, she returned to her phone conversation. "I don't care! Two for five! Then put Father Patrick on! Put Father Patrick on!"

The door slammed shut in Emily's face. She raised her fist to knock a second time. Perhaps she could persuade Loretta by telling her about the benefits of airing out the stale hallway smell. Just as her hand was about to touch the door, someone grabbed her arm.

"What are you doing?" Jennifer whispered as she let go of Emily.

"If Loretta opens her door, we can get a draft going between our rooms. It will be so much cooler!"

"She's never going to do that!"

"Why not?"

"Because she's *Loretta*! She once pulled the fire alarm because if *she* couldn't sleep, no one could sleep. We all had to stand outside until the fire department arrived. And it was February!"

"She's gotta be hot in there."

"She doesn't care."

Emily stared longingly at the open doors down at the end of the hallway. "But the cool breeze."

"Go sit in one of the air conditioning rooms. At least you know Loretta's up here. She's not going to barge in with her bullshit and open one of the windows because she thinks air conditioning works better with circulation."

"I wish I could go sit in the AC, but I can't," Emily lamented. "I need to finish unpacking."

"I have a tower fan you can borrow for a bit. You can prop it by the window and that will suck in some of the cooler air."

"Yes!"

"But I want it back before bed."

"You're a lifesaver! Thank—"

"Eww!" Jennifer pointed to a cockroach scuttling under Loretta's door. "Look!"

"Was that a cockroach?" Emily said.

"Yes! There was one in my room yesterday. I *knew* it came from Loretta." Jennifer pounded on Loretta's door. "A cockroach just returned to your room!"

"What?" Loretta, incredulous, yelled from inside. "What did you do to bring cockroaches in here?" Seconds later, roach spray poured out from underneath the door. Loretta was spraying the length of the entire crack, back and forth.

"You need to turn that can around, Loretta," Jennifer said, coughing. "It's you, not us!"

"I don't think so," Loretta said as she continued to spray underneath the door until the can was empty. "I take care of everything. This place would be horrible if it wasn't for me!"

EIGHT

When Heather walked into The Zonderling that evening, it was unusually quiet. Unsettlingly quiet. No one was singing, yelling into a phone, or excessively spraying anything. The receptionist, Corporal Kim, waved to Heather. Corporal Kim was thirty years old and had been at The Zonderling for two years. Her mom was a high-ranking member of the Altruistic Army, and Corporal Kim wanted to follow in her mom's footsteps to one day become sergeant major. As the day receptionist, Corporal Kim's main duties were handling mail, answering the phone, and stopping guys from sneaking in the building. Her overnight counterpart, Corporal Steve, spent nearly 100 percent of his job dedicated to the latter.

"Perfect timing, getting home," Corporal Kim said. "The residents' meeting just started. It's in the cafetorium."

The cafetorium was on the ground floor of The Zonderling. It had a stage at one end and dining tables spread throughout the room. A small balcony, connected to the second-floor music room, overlooked the space. Free concerts, courtesy of those practicing in the music room, ranged from delightful to unbearable, depending on the skill of the musician in question.

Over the years, resident musicians, actors, and dancers performed in concerts, plays, and talent shows in the cafetorium. Many illustrious performers had graced its stage, like 1950s German resident Sigrid Fuß who went on to spend the sixties dancing (i.e. stripping) in the finest clubs in Las Vegas. Actress Hazel DeVries had also performed in one Flag Day talent show before rising to fame in multiple 1980s comedies where she always played the girlfriend of a preppy, country club jerk who got his comeuppance from the scrappy, party-hardy leading man.

The cafetorium used to be an auditorium, and there was a separate dining room next door. But during the aerobics craze, residents convinced management that there was a dire need for a gym where residents could dance around in stretchy neon fabric. After the purchase of a few Richard Simmons and Jane Fonda tapes, the auditorium became a cafetorium, and the dining room became a gym. The only problem was that the dumbwaiter remained in the gym, which meant that it carried food from the basement kitchen straight to the exercise room. Staff then loaded food onto a cart and wheeled it through the lobby and into the cafetorium for meals. As a result the gym usually smelled like fried chicken, scrambled eggs, and sweat. It was an odor best known to parents everywhere as *teenage boy*.

The residents' meeting was already in progress, so Heather quietly walked into the cafetorium. The quarterly meetings were meant to inform residents of changes, fun activities, and housing issues. They always went one of two ways: short and to the point, or long and painful. If just one long-term resident turned up, it would quickly spiral into a two-hour ordeal about nothing, especially if Loretta was present. As it was, eighty-five-year-old Helen usually spent fifteen minutes at every meeting complaining about a food conspiracy—she used to get *four* of something (potatoes, carrots, tomatoes, etc.) at dinner, but now she only got *three*.

Heather entered just as Helen finished her tirade about the salad bar and the alarming invasion of garbanzo beans. Emily waved for Heather to join her and Jennifer at a table.

"Thank you, Helen," The General said. "We will keep that in mind next time we decide to add anything with a name that sounds like garbage."

"No one wants garbage beans," Helen moaned. "Bring back the bacon bits!"

"Duly noted," The General said.

Heather sat down next to Jennifer. "Thanks for the seat."

"No problem," Jennifer said. "You have a leaf stuck in your hair."

Panic stricken, Heather reached up and pulled a small leaf out of her dark blonde hair. She was relieved when she discovered it was stuck to the clump of hair that was tacky from the subway slime. *Thank God it wasn't there during my job interview.*

"How did the temp thing go? You get a job?" Emily asked.

"I got something at International Bank! I mean, it's not on Wall Street, but it's international!"

"That's awesome!"

"What department?" Jennifer asked. "I know some people there."

"The NRI department."

"Never heard of it. Are you sure it's called *NRI?*"

"Yes, because I was thinking it sounded like a Cockney person saying *Henry*. If you pronounced NRI like a name."

"Like 'enry!" Emily said.

"Yeah!"

"Like 'enry 'iggins!" Emily said with a Dick Van Dyke English accent. "Oi, guv'nah! Apples and pears! That's *stairs* to you Yanks!"

"Quiet down, everyone, so we can finish. Next on the agenda," The General said as he looked at his list. "The laundry room."

A woman stood up. Despite the heat, she was wearing jeans, a short-sleeved plaid shirt, and a slouchy knit hat.

"That's Stinky Carrie," Jennifer whispered. "I don't know how she keeps her receptionist job. That BO is quite a 'Welcome to our office.'"

"Washer number three," Stinky Carrie said. "When is it getting replaced? It's had an out-of-order sign on it forever."

"This is news to me! Did you fill out a work order to fix it?" The General said.

"No, because there's already an out-of-order sign on it."

"I think that was someone just trying to be neighborly by letting you know it was broken. Save you a few quarters on a bad machine."

"Or someone using a fake sign to keep the machine to themselves," Jennifer said under her breath. She'd noticed that washer number three always worked when Loretta was in the laundry room.

"Are you going to fix it?" Stinky Carrie asked as the entire room silently cheered on her apparent newfound interest in clean clothes.

"Yes. Once protocol is followed, and you fill out a work order for Captain David."

"But I'm reporting it now."

"Written orders lead to marching orders in the Altruistic Army."

"That's such a stupid waste of time because I have to pick up a work order from *you*."

"Between the hours of nine a.m. and five p.m."

"When I'm working! How am I supposed—"

"Enough about the washing machine!" Loretta shouted as she stood up. "We need to focus on the real problem."

"Loretta, you know you're always last on the agenda," The General said in vain.

Undeterred, Loretta continued. "The real problem is that a person or several persons are perpetrating heinous crimes in the twelfth-floor bathroom, and they need to be punished."

Jennifer rolled her eyes. "You mean like the shower you're squatting in? You can't keep personal items in the bathroom, Loretta. No one wants to see your underwear."

"That's very true," The General said. "Anyone keeping things in the bathrooms should remove them. Moving along to the next item—"

Completely ignoring The General, Loretta continued. "First, the entire sink area is always a mess of water and soap. Especially the area between the sink and soap dispensers."

"A normal thing that happens when people wash their hands," Jennifer muttered to Emily and Heather. "Something she knows nothing about."

"Second, there are always paper towels on the floor."

"Because you're hoarding them in a shower stall," Jennifer said loudly. "The breeze from the window blows them around."

"Someone is going to slip and fall on the paper towels, and then you just wait for the lawsuit to pay the medical bills," Loretta said in a patronizing voice. "And third, speaking of paper, there is never any toilet paper in the morning."

"We restock it every day," The General said.

"It doesn't matter!" Loretta said. "All these young people and foreigners. They don't care about keeping this place clean! Or people who just don't care about anything in general, like Martha! The toilet seats are always a complete mess from her hovering!"

"Since we're discussing toilet paper, stop wasting money on two-ply," Helen said as she stood up. "Get one-ply and use the extra money for more bacon bits!"

"Hold on, Helen," Loretta said. "I think we can get bacon bits back without sacrificing the two-ply. Sit down." Helen obeyed, and Loretta continued. "We're not switching to that coarse one-ply, General."

The General was eager for the meeting to end. "We can leave the two-ply toilet paper as is."

"Good," Loretta said. "But it barely scratches the surface of the problems around here."

"You mean like the cockroaches in your room?" Jennifer said.

"*Allegedly*. No one has seen them except you," Loretta said.

"Emily saw them too."

"This is exactly why I buy my own roach poison. Management never does anything!"

"Management can't do anything if management doesn't know," The General said. "I wonder what's changed. There hasn't been a pest problem in quite some time."

"That's because I take care of it," Loretta said. "I take care of everything!"

"I'll have Captain David look into it." The General didn't want to hear any more about it because he had to get to the library by 1900 hours to help Lieutenant Rachel alphabetize the books. Lieutenant Rachel disliked tardiness as much as she disliked F. Scott Fitzgerald on the shelf next to J. K.

Rowling. If The General didn't get to the second floor soon, he knew that his favorite Grisham novels would temporarily disappear into Lieutenant Rachel's locked office. He looked at his watch. "Meeting adjourned."

Emily whispered to Heather and Jennifer, "You know Loretta's right about the toilet paper. There wasn't any in the bathroom this morning."

"Shhh! Don't give her the satisfaction!" Jennifer said. "I told you to always bring emergency tissues."

"Methinks the lady doth protest too much," Emily said.

"Exactly!" Jennifer said. "Loretta complains about things being gross, but only does it to divert attention."

"She kind of treats this place like it's her own house instead of a shared community," Heather said.

"And then acts like the self-appointed arbiter of the whole building. The Zonderling has its quirks, but it's not bad," Jennifer said. "It's people like Loretta that make it worse."

"She actually broke the bathroom fan because she didn't like the setting I had it on," Heather said.

"Once she refused to replace the batteries in her beeping smoke alarm because she wanted to annoy someone into moving out," Jennifer said.

"Couldn't maintenance just enter her room and fix it?"

"She barricaded the door and yelled about the Constitution. The General gave up, and the girl moved out."

"What did she do to Loretta?"

"I heard she braved the elements and used Loretta's shower once because all of the others were occupied," Jennifer said. "Loretta's like a cockroach. She'll survive anything and is impossible to eliminate."

"I can't believe she won't open her door to create a draft in this heat," Emily said. "You know what? I'm not helping her take her garbage outside anymore."

"Why are you doing that anyway?" Jennifer asked. "She should just be putting it in the main garbage in the bathroom that maintenance empties."

"She always has too much stuff to put in there."

"Maybe Loretta's cleaning out her disgusting room and disturbed the cockroaches hiding there."

"Nasty," Emily said. "But I'd believe it. From what I could see in her room, she has floor-to-ceiling piles of—"

"Napkins?" Heather asked as she gestured to Loretta and Helen who were filling their pockets with napkins from the dispensers on the tables.

"Maybe," Emily said.

"What is it with her and paper products?" Jennifer said.

"It looked more like a pile of wrenches."

"Isn't that what The General was worried about?" Heather asked.

"Flag Day," Emily said as she nodded.

"Did I tell you that she trapped me in the bathroom yesterday?" Jennifer said. "The one downstairs by the lobby."

"How did she do that?" Heather and Emily simultaneously asked, purely out of trying to make sure they didn't become Loretta's next victims.

Jennifer told Emily and Heather about how she had been working on her computer in the parlor. Even though she'd been there so long that her computer was getting hot on her lap, it was a million times more comfortable to be in the air-conditioned TV room during the late afternoon instead of in her tiny, hot room.

Suddenly Loretta walked in, refreshed from her post-afternoon-talk-show nap. In preparation for the inevitable barrage of cable news that would surely appear on the TV, Jennifer turned up the volume on the music playing in her headphones. But Loretta didn't go for the remote. She went straight to the closed window next to the window AC unit—and opened the window.

Jennifer glared at Loretta with a glare of a thousand suns—the kind of glare that prompts immediate confessions from guilty small children and husbands.

"The air conditioner will overheat if the window is closed," Loretta said.

As Loretta sat on the couch, Jennifer rose from her chair with her laptop. With one swift move, she walked to the window, slammed it shut, and sat down in the chair in front of it.

"It's ninety-nine degrees outside!" Jennifer snapped.

Three cable news rants later, nature called and Jennifer went to the bathroom near the cafetorium. After washing her hands, she tried to open the door, but it wouldn't move. She bent down to look under the door and saw four skinny metal legs.

"Dammit, Loretta!" Jennifer yelled as she shook the handle. "Open the door! And stop stealing Martha's walker!"

"Wait, wait, wait!" Heather said, interrupting Jennifer. "I saw Loretta with the walker yesterday! It was right when I first walked in the door!"

"Probably on her way to wedge it under the door handle so that she could open the window without the judgment of common sense," Jennifer said.

"Loretta even threatened me. Told me not to say anything. Twice!"

"She's the worst. If she wants swamp ass, then she can go to her room!" Jennifer was nearly hyperventilating because she was so mad. "There are only three rooms in this sweat box that have air conditioning, which is why we call them *air conditioning rooms!*"

"Why doesn't The Zonderling kick her out?" Heather asked.

"No one ever gets kicked out," Jennifer moaned. "The General would have to catch her red-handed as she cut the cord to his TV just before his favorite show."

It was nearly impossible to get evicted from The Zonderling, unless one was caught with a guy or suspected of being a Communist. A Communist-based eviction had only happened once when a resident refused to watch or cheer for America during the Miracle on Ice game because she was a poet who just didn't care about ice hockey.

"Let's complain to The General. He'll make her stop," Emily said.

"Believe me, everyone complains about her, but it doesn't make a difference. Besides, how can The General police her nasty personal behavior? Especially in the bathroom. It's impossible. She always just throws Martha under the bus anyway."

"Why?" Heather asked.

"I don't know. Martha probably grabbed the remote out of Loretta's claws or something," Jennifer said. "That's why it sucks. You don't want to live with her asinine behavior, but you also don't want to complain and become the next Martha."

"I definitely believe Loretta would do something gross to my food," Heather said.

"Hey, how did you get out of the bathroom when she trapped you with the walker?" Emily asked Jennifer.

"The General found me when the fire alarm went off. *Merci* to the French girls for smoking."

NINE

The lobby of International Bank was just as Heather dreamed it would be. It gleamed of luxurious everything. And it was just so...*international.* So many foreign accents! So many cuff links! So many power cigars on their way to be smoked outside!

Everyone looked like they just stepped out of a fashion magazine photo spread. Well, everyone except Heather. Her suit was one size too big, and she probably over accessorized, but it didn't matter because she felt fabulous, even though she had to cover her feet in blister bandages on the walk from the subway to the office. *Now I get why women wore ugly sneakers to work in all those New York movies,* Heather thought.

The lobby was particularly spotless that morning because that's what happens when a building manager tells the overnight janitorial staff to scrub the lobby until it's spotless. Yesterday International Bank had held its first annual volunteer fair for employees. It went as well as could be expected in a building full of wannabe wolves of Wall Street. The company only held the volunteer fair to get some new tax credit anyway. The bank's Corporate Responsibility and Purpose department knew it would be a challenge to get anyone to show up to an event with the word *volunteer* in the name, let alone commit to reading to school kids or picking up trash in the park. They needed something flashy to get bodies in the lobby.

After a lap-dance lunch brainstorming session, the sharp minds in the CRAP team developed a surefire plan to get employees involved. And any surefire plan for employees at International Bank required one thing: booze. The CRAP department hired a team of bartenders to mix up the trendiest vodka cocktails and then advertised the drinks in the company-wide e-mail about the volunteer fair. The head of CRAP made sure that the font size of the fair headline was no more than four points smaller than the free vodka headline. She had principles, after all, being head of the charitable arm of an international investment bank and everything.

Of the employees who were allowed to leave their desks, five out of five attended the event. The CRAP team managed to get over 85 percent of attendees to sign up for something, which represented a tremendous success for the volunteer fair. Bonuses all around for the CRAP team! Technically, all employees had to follow through on their volunteer commitment, regardless of their drunken state when signing up. If they didn't, they'd get demerits on their annual reviews. However, demerits were something only HR considered a threat, meaning that just 23 percent of sign-ups actually did any volunteering. Employees knew they would never receive a bad performance review if they brought in money—not even if they doused the lobby plants in vodka and lit them on fire during a volunteer fair. To be fair to the foreign exchange team, the flaming plants *did* kind of look like tiki torches at a luau.

As Heather rode the glass elevator up to the twenty-fourth floor, she noticed with awe that there was a television above the button panel. With live TV! An earnest female anchor was reporting the very important news that SoDeDyFa Sushi had acquired a shipment of specialty bluefin tuna. The anchor urgently told viewers that they should immediately call the restaurant to enter the reservation lottery for a chance at tasting the fish.

The General stood at The Zonderling's reception desk and was watching the same news report about the SoDeDyFa bluefin.

"I just don't get it," he said to Corporal Kim, who was busy playing a game on her phone. "Raw fish is food poisoning. Why would you ever enter a lottery for food poisoning?"

"Some people have more money than sense, sir," Corporal Kim said.

The General spotted Emily entering the building. "Miss Benson! How are you today?"

"Morning, General! Just got back from a super basic-training workshop," Emily said. "It was a boot camp for improv basics."

"I remember my first day of boot camp," The General said as he began to fondly reminisce about his salad days, or as he liked to jokingly call them, his *soup days.* "I was so nervous that I spilled an entire box of oyster crackers at the soup kitchen. And then I ended up with clam chowder all over my uniform after ignoring my commanding officer's advice on ladling technique."

"Oh no! You can't ignore proper ladling!"

"The crackers and chowder were just the start of it! I'm still haunted by my first Thanksgiving at the soup kitchen when I was in charge of the gravy boat. I'm an army man, not a navy man!"

The new International Bank building opened in midtown five years ago. The company prided itself on erecting such an environmentally friendly building in the heart of New York City, something the International Bank PR department mentioned in every press release. The former headquarters had been closer to Wall Street, but the board wanted to take the company into the new millennium with a flashy, high-tech base that was closer to the cameras of morning news shows and tourists. Luckily there was an old building that was easy to demolish once International Bank wrote a check with so many zeros that it looked like it was from a children's cartoon.

The building that International Bank purchased had been originally built for the Chivalrous Order of the Benevolent Lambda Lambs after the destruction of their first club in the Thanksgiving Horse Stampede of 1897. When the Benevolent Lambda Lambs dissolved during the Great Depression, the building was turned into an elaborate Hawaiian-themed movie palace similar to the Chinese or Egyptian theaters in Hollywood. Many extravagant film premieres were held at the Hawaiian before the owners converted it to a live TV studio during the golden age of television. Countless actors and musicians graced the stage at the Hawaiian as they made American cultural history. But unfortunately the Hawaiian Theater had no Jackie Kennedy Onassis to its Grand Central Terminal. After International Bank made an unthinkable offer for the location and the air rights—because in New York City, people actually bought and sold air for millions of dollars—wrecking balls descended upon the Hawaiian like a tsunami.

To be fair, International Bank did save the "Aloha! Welcome to the Hawaiian!" sign and placed it in their lobby for selfie-stick-toting tourists. There was also a really expensive plaque outside of the building explaining the site's history of Benevolent Lambda Lambs and movie stars. So it was all good as far as International Bank was concerned. Ironically the founders of International Bank, the Biancarini brothers, had been active members of the Benevolent Lambda Lambs. They had closed many important business deals in the smoking room of the now-destroyed fraternal headquarters. The board of International Bank was certain that the Biancarini brothers would be cool with demolishing their beloved club in the name of twenty-first-century commerce.

Far above the Aloha lobby, Heather briskly followed her new supervisor, Vikram Singh, through a quiet department bull pen on the twenty-fourth floor. Everyone looked very busy as they quickly typed in silence. But in fact, as is the case with a roomful of quiet employees, no one was actually working on real work. They couldn't make calls because they were too busy complaining via online chat about a colleague's smelly perfume. To be fair, some were working really hard on pitching an official hashtag for the stink bomb situation, and the top three contenders were #EauDeCorpseFlower, #AttackoftheKillerGardenias, and #TheHangover2.

"You'll also be doing daily package pickup for the entire NRI department, of which I am in charge," Vikram said. "So don't let me catch you staring out the window at the 'big buildings,' or crying on the phone to your mom because New Yorkers are 'so mean.'"

The Bluetooth on Vikram's ear began flashing. Born and raised in New Jersey, thirty-eight-year-old Vikram never got out of bed without his Bluetooth in his ear, his twenty-four-karat-gold bracelet on his wrist, or his hair properly gelled. And just in case there was a gel crisis at work, he had an emergency five-hundred-milliliter jar of his salon's bespoke gel on his desk next to his dying bonsai tree.

Vikram raised his hand to the Bluetooth device and answered the call. "Go for Vik." He immediately ignored Heather and began arguing in Hindi.

As Vikram talked, Heather noticed a large framed ad for International Bank that hung on the wall: "Number One in Nonresident Indian Accounts. Send money home to India with an NRI from International Bank." Heather looked around her new workplace. It was an open floor plan, so she could see everyone. And nearly everyone in the NRI department was Indian. *Nonresident Indian. Well, now I know what NRI means*, she thought.

Banks around the world started Nonresident Indian departments when they realized that professionals were emigrating from India for high-paying jobs abroad. Nothing excited banks more than creating a product that would generate a new revenue stream. These NRI accounts would allow Indian expats in places like the United States, the United Kingdom, and Canada to easily send money to family back home. Bank executives salivated over the additional revenue from account fees. The pivot tables on their new monthly spreadsheets looked *very* impressive. Bonus-worthy impressive.

One of those executives was Vikram, who loved nothing more than seeing numbers increase when he refreshed a pivot table. It was the third most satisfying part of his day, after tracking packages online and receiving the morning fashion text from his UK counterpart, Humphrey. Vikram and The Humpster were very impressed with the expensive sartorial choices of the young, new VP of NRI titanium accounts, Sir Julian Frostbite of Wibbly Dibblyshire. Sir Julian had so much classy style that he would never stoop to wearing the same cuff links twice. Vikram had recently been in London to meet Sir Julian and complimented the cuff links when they were having an after-work pint. Sir Julian immediately gave them to Vikram as he no longer had any need for used accessories. From that day forward, The Humpster sent cuff-link-of-the-day photos to Vikram (unless they were cuff links that The Humpster wanted for himself). Each morning Vikram usually spent several minutes looking up the cuff link brand online to figure out which ones were worth asking for. This really pissed off his wife, who had to get three teenage boys showered, dressed, and out of the house at the same time as their father.

Since Vikram was an important executive, he insisted that his kids attend an important private school in Manhattan even though none of their New Jersey neighborhood friends went there. Sir Julian had recommended Upper Crustington Academy because his foxhunting pal's sister's husband's stepson was a current student. One day, in his dream of dreams, Vikram wanted to go on a foxhunt with the Frostbites of Wibbly Dibblyshire, so being associated with the right school would definitely help his chances. Vikram dropped off his kids every day at Upper Crustington in his newly leased luxury car before arriving at the International Bank building. Vikram, on account of being an important executive, was able to park in the underground executive garage for important executives who were too important to use public transportation.

But even an important executive like Vikram wasn't immune to phone calls from his irate wife. Today she was berating him for forgetting their sons' lunches on the kitchen counter. Vikram profusely apologized to his wife—in Hindi, so Heather wouldn't understand—and ended the call. He turned back to Heather and said, "Crisis in the Mumbai office. Where was I?"

"You're Vikram, and you're very important."

"Exactly. And you're just a temp. With a weird accent."

Heather followed him to a group of desks whose occupants included a guy and a cute Indian woman whose fashion icon appeared to be early-era Snooki.

"You're next to Mira," Vikram said as he pointed to Indian Snooki.

"Hi! Welcome to the NRI!" Mira said, shaking Heather's hand. "Before you sit down, let me clean off your desk. It's still really sticky. Nick spilled on it again and never cleaned it up." She grabbed paper towels and cleaner from her desk drawer.

"Thanks, Mira," Heather said. *See, Heather! New Yorkers are nice.*

Vikram's Bluetooth blinked again. Being very important, he immediately answered it. "Hold for Vik." He looked at Heather and said, "I need to deal with this." He then turned to the guy and said, "Hey, Nick, explain account reconciliation to the temp."

As Vikram walked away, he shouted into his Bluetooth, "Bro, those tiki torches of yours were epic!"

The guy spun around in his chair. When his eyes landed on Heather, he immediately yelled, "Granny Panties!"

Holy shit! It's Nick the Dick.

Heather's mind flashed back to elementary school recess when she was nine years old. She had been proudly shoving a carrot into her finished snowman when Nick ran over to her, laughing like Jack Nicholson in *Batman*. "There is no Santa Claus!" he screamed as he knocked off the snowman's head. He ran away, continuing to yell, "There is no Santa Claus!" All of the kindergartners cried.

She flashed forward seven years to high school study hall and saw Nick launch tiny spitballs into the hair of the oblivious girl sitting in front of him. He caught Heather staring. As soon as she looked away, three spitballs hit Heather's cheek in quick succession.

And then she thought about the time in the school hallway, one month later. After observing Heather exit the bathroom, Nick very helpfully informed his jock friends that she had accidentally tucked her skirt into her tights. "I see London, I see France, I see Heather's granny underpants!"

Heather snapped back to the present when a camera flash exploded in her face. Nick quickly typed on his phone as he talked to himself. "Granny Panties is my new temp. And *post.*"

TEN

Emily sat on the stoop of The Zonderling and took a selfie with a magazine that she'd just purchased at the newsstand around the corner. None of her friends in Whynot, North Dakota, would believe that there was a whole magazine filled with auditions. Real ones! Not just auditions for snowmobile commercials. Back home Emily was the face of the most popular snowmobile retailer in central North Dakota. Her biggest ad was one where she wore a tank top and blaze orange snow pants, straddled a snowmobile, and said, "Don't trust those brand-new sleds. Only Snow Bob's *Used* Snowmobiles are guaranteed to work again after they've crashed through the ice!"

The newsstand on the corner of New Holland Circle and Limburg Street was the first newsstand she had ever seen in real life. It was just like the movies! Getting cash from the ATM next door was the first time that she'd ever seen an ATM vestibule in real life. It was just like the one that

Chandler got stuck inside! And ordering coffee from the shop across the street also marked the first time that she'd walked out of a coffee shop because there was no way she was going to pay those prices for coffee unless it was poured by Prince Harry. It was a real morning of firsts for Emily.

As Emily posted the magazine selfie, a hot guy in his thirties approached and handed a DVD to her. "Hey there!" he said. "We've been filming a movie, and you've been so fantastic in the background that you deserve a DVD of the scene."

"OMG! I just moved here to be an actress!"

"I knew it!" the man said, with a megawatt smile. "Here, give that back to me and I'll write down the timecode of your scene. What's your name?"

If Emily had thought about this scenario for a minute, she probably would have seen right through the con man's scheme. But all she heard in her head was, "You're in a New York movie!"

Before Emily could respond, someone grabbed the DVD case from her hand. The interloper tossed it back at the con man and yelled, "No, no, no, no, no! It's a scam!"

"Careful! That's my scene!" Emily said. She turned around and saw Jennifer, who had just arrived at The Zonderling after finishing work.

"Come on!" Jennifer demanded. "Do you see a camera? Do you see teamsters? Do you see me screaming at production assistants about my right to walk down this sidewalk whenever I want?"

"No," Emily admitted. "But I do see the actress playing the tuppence-a-bag lady."

Jennifer turned to look where Emily was pointing, which was at a homeless woman who was sitting on a nearby stoop and talking to pigeons.

"I saw *Mary Poppins* nineteen times before it went back into the Disney vault," Emily said. "Look at that lady and her birds. Method acting. Respect."

Good God! "This guy's a con man!" Jennifer said. "He writes your name on the DVD then harasses you for money because it's 'personalized' and can't be resold."

Jennifer could see the wheels turning very slowly in Emily's mind. "Emily, this is New York," she continued. "Everything has a catch: a hello, a seat on the train, a coupon for a free massage. Say no, be aggressive, push tourists..."

While Jennifer dispensed advice, the con man wrote *Emily* on the DVD. "*Emily,*" he said. "That will be fifty dollars."

Emily grabbed the DVD. "So cool!"

"Are you kidding me?" Jennifer wheeled around to face him.

"She took possession. I want my money."

"Oh, you want your money? I just saw a cop around the corner. I'm sure she can help you. Should I go get her? The *cop?*"

Jennifer and the con man stared each other down. After a beat he took off running in the opposite direction.

"That's right!" Jennifer screamed. "Run all the way back to Times Square, where I look forward to busting your fake-sailor-uniform-wearing ass next Fleet Week!"

"Speaking of Times Square," Emily said, "those free stress tests on the street are a real bargain!"

"Tell me you didn't buy—"

Emily held up several science fiction books.

"You bought five of them."

"They said these books really eliminate stress."

"Those aren't just sci-fi books, Emily. Those weren't even real stress tests. Those people were from—"

"And someone else gave me a coupon for a free medical massage! How cool is that? Do you want to come with? He said I could bring more people as long as they were girls."

"OK. You need to learn the most important thing that I learned after I arrived here from Minnesota—the NYFU face."

Emily's face fell. "Should I have asked for more coupons? Darn it! I should have asked for more coupons!"

Eleven

Back at International Bank, Heather couldn't believe that the bane of her childhood was at her new job. "What are you doing here, Nick?" Heather grabbed a chair and sat down at her freshly cleaned desk.

"I'm your new boss, Granny Panties!" Nick said. "I'm the NRI team leader!" Looking for a high five, he turned to Mira. "Team NRI!"

"I told you that I'm never touching your hands again," Mira said.

"That was one time!" Nick protested.

"Like that makes it better."

Nick rolled his eyes and then high-fived himself. "Go team!" His phone beeped, and he looked at the message. "Hey, Big Mike wants to know if you're still wearing granny panties."

"But why are you in New York?" Heather asked. "I thought you were in Florida."

Upon high school graduation, Nick famously went to college in Florida in order to maximize time spent with beer, boobs, and foreign tourist boobs.

"Yeah, Florida was awesome! Spring break every day." He swiveled his chair to look at Mira. "Hashtag *international stank!*"

"Love it! That's so much easier to type than the one about the killer gardenias," Mira said. She opened the chat window on her computer and added *#InternationalStank* as a contender for the official incident hashtag along with *#GrannyPerfume*.

Nick turned back to Heather. "I moved up to New York for my MBA."

They stared at each other until Nick's phone beeped again, breaking the awkward stillness. "Silence speaks volumes, Granny Panties!" He laughed and answered the message. "Yes, she is," he said.

"What is happening?" Heather said to herself.

"What is happening is you are blowing up!" Nick said as he scrolled through new alerts on his phone. "You want to see?"

"No!" Mira yelled to Heather. "Don't ever look directly at his phone! It's like an eclipse. Whatever image is on there will be burned into your eyes forever."

"Come on, Mira!" Nick said. "Vik thought that was hilarious! So did everyone else. I got a zillion likes on that photo."

"Was that before or after your mom commented on it?"

"Shut up, Mira."

"She's never sending your aunt's homemade honey to you ever again."

Nick's phone beeped several more times. "Yo, Granny Panties! Stand up and turn around. Jockstrap wants a photo of your ass. And so does Link, Pubes, and Mr. Hauser from math class."

"No. What's wrong with you?" Heather said, looking around for an escape. "I'm thirsty. Where's the bubbler?"

"*Bubbler?* Oh my God, you're in New York now."

"No, I meant..." *What's the word? WHAT'S THE WORD?!* "...I'd like some water."

Nick was totally absorbed with his beeping phone. "There's no *drinking fountain*, but Mira can take you to the kitchen. Take her to the kitchen, Mira."

"You know what, Nick?" Mira said. "I'm not going to give you a hard time about forgetting to say *please*, because Heather clearly has years of gossip on you that she can share with me."

Nick looked up from his phone. "Wait, what did you just say?"

"Nothing." Mira turned to Heather and said, "The kitchen is right this way."

Heather began following Mira and then realized that her back was toward Nick's phone. She awkwardly alternated walking backward and forward, pretending to notice office décor, as she stumbled around behind Mira. Meanwhile,

Nick still managed to photograph Heather's ass, a post that Mr. Hauser *liked* immediately.

While Heather dealt with a nightmare from her past at work, Emily was learning NYFU lessons for the future in Jennifer's room at The Zonderling.

"Stop making eye contact!" Jennifer said.

"But—"

"No! Do it again."

Emily got up from the bed, walked to the door, turned around, and walked back over to the bed where Jennifer was sitting with her purse next to her. Emily looked at Jennifer and said, "Excuse me, can you move..."

Jennifer rolled her eyes, picked up her bag, and put it on her lap without looking at Emily. Emily sat next to her and, with a smile, said, "Thanks so much!"

"No! What are you doing? Don't talk to anyone on the subway! I'm the jerk who had my stuff on the seat in a crowded train."

"But you moved it."

"That's not the point."

"I don't know. I was nice, so you moved it."

"Forget about the bag," Jennifer said. "You're now on the subway."

"Right."

"Can I ask you a question about your hair? You have great hair!"

"Thank you so much!"

"Ignore me, Emily."

"But you gave me a compliment."

"No, I didn't. I'm trying to get you to come to my shady salon where I'll charge you a fortune and then rope you into some knockoff purse scam."

"But—"

"No! Anyone who *asks* to ask you a question is trying to con you. A tourist with a real question just asks the question. They don't ask if they can ask you how to get to Central Park."

"Huh?"

"Tourists just say, 'How do I get to Central Park?'"

"How *do* I get to Central Park from here?"

"Focus!"

"OK."

"Can I ask you a question about your hair?"

Emily didn't say anything, but she turned and smiled at Jennifer.

"What are you doing? That's engaging! And what do we do?"

"Never engage."

"Never engage! No smiling, no eye contact!"

"But you're talking to me."

"Stare straight ahead into the window, right between the two people sitting in front of you."

Emily looked ahead with a little smile on her face.

"Did you make eye contact?"

"Sorry."

"Read the advertising, that's what it's there for."

Emily still had a small smile on her face.

"Stop smiling! What are you smiling at? The ad for a sleazy ambulance-chasing attorney? There's nothing to ever smile about on the subway."

Jennifer squished Emily's mouth with one hand to remove her smile, but it bounced right back like rubber.

"Stop it!"

"I'm trying!"

Jennifer realized that she needed her other hand to squish Emily's midwestern smile to death. "Keep your face like this. Stare dead ahead. No matter what happens. Dead eyes, Emily!"

"Like when you're trying to pretend that you didn't smell Mr. Mulveney farting at the school bake sale?"

"I have no idea, but sure. Just keep the dead eyes. Stare at the ads." Jennifer removed her hands from Emily's face. "OK, you're getting there. Scowl more, like Mr. Mulveney farted *and* took the last chocolate chip cookie bar."

Emily, dead eyes straight ahead, gave a thumbs-up.

"Can I ask you a question about your hair?"

The corner of Emily's mouth twitched, but otherwise she successfully maintained her newfound NYFU face.

"Good," Jennifer said. "Now a mariachi band just got on the train and—"

Emily's face lit up. "I love live music!"

Jennifer groaned and put her face into her hands. "*NYFU, Emily! NYFU!*"

Safely away from Nick, Heather downed a glass of water from the most expensive water purifier that she'd ever seen. The NRI department kitchen was huge. It even had a refrigerator filled with free expensive energy drinks. The International Bank team of efficiency experts felt that an endless supply of non-FDA-approved energy drinks was worth the cost because "energized" employees worked much longer hours.

Mira hadn't taken an energy drink, but that didn't stop her from talking a mile a minute in her Brooklyn accent.

"I can't believe you went to school with Nick! What a small world. It's just like when I was in the Bronx and ran into Ana Rodriguez from PS 444K321 in Brooklyn. I'm like, 'What are you doing here?' and she's like, 'What are *you* doing here?' Then we were both like, 'I fell asleep on the subway again!'" Mira laughed. "Lived here my whole life and the only reason I ever end up in the Bronx is because I fall asleep on the two train."

Heather nodded, but she didn't understand any of Mira's references. Just as Heather was about to ask about the meaning of a *PS 444K321*, Nick burst into the kitchen. He was holding a package and staring at Heather.

"Why is this in my hand?" Nick asked.

"Well, Nick," Heather said. "Under the laws of physics—"

"I know you just got off the bus, but what don't you understand about package pickup deadlines?"

"I don't know what you're talking about. No one told me anything about package pickup deadlines."

"And what don't you understand about picking up packages from department heads?" Nick continued. "If you can't do your job, I'm afraid we're going to have to let you go." In between playing games on his phone, Nick excelled at telling other people what to do. It was one of the many transferrable skills that he picked up at his New York MBA class.

"No one told me any of this!" *You jerk.*

Nick looked at the large, shiny watch that he wore to make sure that others knew how much money he pretended to make. "You have ten minutes to take this to the store before it closes."

She didn't know where she was going, but she knew she had only ten minutes. Heather grabbed the package and dashed into the hallway, trying to look up the address on her phone as she ran.

Nick stepped into the hall and yelled after her. "You're in New York now, Granny Panties! Get your act together!"

Snap! He took another photo of her ass as she ran away. As he looked at the picture on his phone, he noticed that Mira was bending over a table while she sorted through gossip magazines. *Why not?* Nick thought. *Snap!*

TWELVE

"Heather. Heather!" Jennifer said as she waved her hand over the phone that occupied all of Heather's attention. They were holding up the dinner line at The Zonderling, and the danger of being stuck at a table with Porn Lisa or Benjamin Button was increasing.

"What? Sorry," Heather said as she put the phone into her pocket. "I've had a lot of messages from random high school people today." Including five "what up?" messages from Pubes and an ignored friend request from Mr. Hauser.

"I said, you shouldn't take the spaghetti," Jennifer said. "Lamb en croute is the way to go."

"How can The Zonderling ruin spaghetti and meatballs?" Heather asked as she scanned the dinner options in the cafetorium.

"Trust me. If it's an old-school meat wrapped in pastry, it's the best option."

Like much of The Zonderling, the chefs were in a time warp of midcentury recipes for cooking—why change when you have perfection? The General certainly did not want to mess with something like the classic recipe for vegetable soup that called for *number 2* cans of corn or *number 303* cans of sliced carrots. However, he did concede to posting a size conversion chart after a new cook used 303 individual cans of sliced carrots in what The General called "a dark day in the history of vegetable soup."

After Heather and Jennifer filled their trays with lamb en croute, mint jelly, and a side salad, they sat down at one of the tables. Each table had a vase with fresh daisies. Someone in the second-floor music room was playing a violin, and it actually sounded good. Heather thought it all seemed pretty fancy until she saw Loretta using her bare hands to scoop feta cheese from the salad bar.

"OK, so these two guys you have to work with—" Jennifer said.

"Nick and Vikram. Nick is the one I went to school with."

"They sound like classic finance bros. You aren't going to get anywhere with them if you're nice to them."

"But Vikram is in charge of the whole department, and Nick reports to him. I can't be mean."

"Mean? It's not being mean. It's about being a New Yorker. You have to keep hitting the ball back into their court with the same intensity."

Unfiltered aggression was the key to survival and respect in New York City, much like passive aggressive niceness was the key to survival and respect in the Midwest. New Yorkers preferred creating confrontation to deal with an issue, whereas midwesterners preferred hate-baking a cake without adding enough vanilla, and giving it to their nemesis with an I-hate-you smile.

"I don't want to get fired. I'm just a temp."

Suddenly a commotion broke out between Loretta and Martha near the salad bar over improper handling of hard-boiled eggs.

"You didn't use tongs!" Loretta yelled.

"Because it was the last hard-boiled egg in the dish," Martha said. "You should talk! We all saw you scoop—"

"Not using tongs at a salad bar is a health hazard. If The General doesn't understand how serious this is, I'll report it to the Department of Health!"

Loretta had reported The Zonderling so many times to the Department of Health that the Department of Health had an ongoing bet as to what her next complaint would be. John Smith, administrative assistant extraordinaire, was in the lead with his remarkable prediction that Loretta would file a complaint about watered-down lime Jell-O. Fifteen days later that complaint arrived on the desk of John's boss.

"Heather," Jennifer said. "If you don't give what you get in New York, no one will ever respect you at work."

The next morning Heather got lost in SoDeDyFa when she had to detour around several new construction sites. Elaborate scaffolding had appeared overnight without explanation and blocked the street signs. No city was as successful at building random scaffolding as New York City.

As Heather finally got her bearings and rounded the corner near the subway station, she was approached by an attractive man holding a serving tray.

"Weed?" the waiter asked.

Taken aback by such a brazen question so early in the morning, Heather stuttered, "What?"

"Weed juice. From dandelions. It's a full-sized sample." The guy was a waiter. He was handing out free samples at the grand opening of a new restaurant named AFWNYC.

Heather looked at the gross dark-green sludge in the small cup that the waiter held for her. "No thanks."

"It's all natural and foraged from the local parks," he continued. "That's what AFW stands for—Artisanal Foraged Weeds."

"You only serve weeds?"

"The best weeds in SoDeDyFa. Sure you don't want to try? Regular price is nine dollars."

"Nine dollars for dandelion juice?"

"Artisanal foraged local dandelions."

"I'm late for work," Heather said. She briskly walked to the subway entrance and ran down the stairs to make the train. Unfortunately she accidentally got on an express subway train instead of a local train because she didn't know that different trains ran on the same track. She missed her stop and arrived thirty minutes late to work.

"I'm sorry! I'm so sorry," Heather babbled as she sat down at her desk. Sweat and makeup poured down her face from running in the New York summer heat.

"We all have train problems. Don't worry about it," Mira said. "Besides, Nick and Vikram have been in line at the coffee shop for the past thirty minutes anyway."

"Thank goodness."

"You want some water? I'm going to the kitchen."

"Yes, thank you!" Mira left for the kitchen, and Heather leaned over to swap her sneakers for work shoes.

"Excuse me," an English voice asked.

Heather sat up and looked at the middle-aged man. "Yes?"

"Do you know where I might find Vikram?"

"No idea."

"*No idea.* Is that still on the ninth floor?"

Heather stared at him like he was an idiot. "I don't know where he is."

"Ha-ha! Is *no idea* on the ninth floor? Good one, Hugh!" Nick said as he arrived with a cup of coffee. Vikram trailed behind, in the middle of another argument in Hindi via Bluetooth because he forgot his son's field trip permission slip on the kitchen table. Nick gestured to Heather. "I think Granny Panties here is always in *no idea.*"

"Right," Hugh said. "Well tell Vikram to come to my office when he's finished."

"No prob, dude. Nice cuff links."

Hugh gave a curt nod to Nick and walked away. Nick turned to Heather. "What's your problem?"

"Me? What's *your* problem?"

"That you didn't laugh at his weird English jokes."

"He didn't say anything funny."

"English people are never funny, Heather. It's called a dry sense of humor."

"*Humour*," Heather said in an English accent. "*O-U-R*."

"No, I'm not. *He's* English."

Heather rolled her eyes. "Never mind."

"And he's the NRI vice president. Vik's boss, Hugh Fletcher."

"He didn't introduce himself."

Vikram ended his call. "What's going on? What did Fletcher want?"

"He was looking for you," Heather said.

"Yeah, man, he said he wanted to see you in his office."

"I bet it's about the new titanium accounts," Vikram said. He looked at Heather, who was wiping sweat off her face. "What's wrong with you? Are you sick? Don't throw up on my shoes! These are thousand-dollar leather shoes that I bought in Italy. In *Firenze*."

"I'm not sick. I had to run from the subway," Heather said. "The red-line train skipped the stop for some reason."

"*Red line*? Stop being such a tourist," Nick said. "It's called the *one*, *two*, or *three* train."

"It's a red line on the map," Heather said.

"Not what it's called," Nick said.

"I don't care what it's called," Vikram said. "I can't believe that you came to work looking like this and now you're sweating all over my department."

"Sorry."

"Why aren't you moving? Go clean yourself up!" Vikram started walking to Hugh's office but stopped and turned around. "Nick, can you go wake up Tanner? He crashed under his desk last night after a bender with a new titanium client. He probably needs a toothbrush and new shirt from the hangover drawer."

Thirteen

When Heather finally left work that night, she boarded the first red-line train that arrived in the station. As she studied the train's subway map to make sure she was on the correct one—and figure out the difference between the one, two, and three trains—a mom leaned over to pick up her toddler's toy. This wouldn't have been an issue except that she was holding a cup of apple juice that was now spilled down Heather's leg.

The walk back to The Zonderling was uncomfortable, sticky, and squishy. As she trudged through humid SoDeDyFa, she walked past a line of excited people that wrapped around the block. They were all standing behind a velvet rope, and there were photographers—the ones who had really long camera lenses—taking photos of the crowd. *Oh my god, it's a celebrity! It's gotta be! My first celebrity sighting!*

Heather approached a fortysomething couple that was in the line. "What's going on? Who's inside?"

"The bluefin," the one man said.

"Is that a band?" Heather asked.

"It's a *tuna*. For sushi." He pointed to the sign that said SoDeDyFa Sushi. "They have a shipment of rare bluefin."

"Don't even bother trying to get in line. All of us already have reservations for tomorrow night," the other man said.

"You're all waiting in line to eat dinner tomorrow night?" *That's the most insane thing I've ever heard.*

"Yes!" the first man said. "It's the *bluefin tuna*."

"Hey!" yelled a middle-aged woman with bright-orange hair. She stood eight people behind the couple who explained the line to Heather. "No cutting!"

"I'm not cutting. I was just asking them—"

"No cutting!"

The people standing near the woman turned and looked at Heather. Their hungry glares threatened sushi-related violence.

"Not cutting! Have a nice dinner everyone!" Heather said as she quickly walked down the block. She briefly paused by the photographers so she could look inside the restaurant to see if there were any celebrities.

"*No cutting!*"

"Welcome home, Heather!" Corporal Kim said. "How was your day today?" Heather was an exhausted, frustrated mess, but it was kind of nice to hear someone welcoming her back.

"Fine. Looking forward to a shower and some sleep."

"Don't forget your mail!" Corporal Kim handed a postcard to Heather. It was from her mom. A photo of the village road sign "Welcome to Poubelle! Population: A whole lotta fun folks!" was on the front. The back of the postcard had a message about some old *Primetime Live* report about muggings. There was also a PS asking how to get a cell phone back to a normal clock after accidentally switching it to military time.

Heather walked over to the elevator and pushed the button. While she waited, a guy in an Altruistic Army uniform briskly walked into the building and breezed past reception.

"Good evening, General," Corporal Kim said. He didn't answer. He just beelined for the elevator. A moment later Corporal Kim yelled, "Security alert! Elevator!"

The General charged out of his office shouting, "Roger! Security alert! Elevator!" He ran through the lobby, pushed past Heather, and threw himself in front of the elevator. "Young man, what you do think you are doing?"

"Crap," the guy muttered. Heather noticed that it was the same guy who had signed in to visit someone when she checked into The Zonderling. He was way too thin to believably pass for The General.

"And in a fake Altruistic Army uniform!" The General said. "It's a federal offense to impersonate an Altruistic Army officer." It wasn't.

"Calm down, dude."

"Your insubordinate behavior has cost you one month of visiting privileges," The General said. "Corporal Kim!"

"On it," Corporal Kim said as she snapped a photo of the guy with her phone.

"Sheesh. I'm leaving, OK? You guys are crazy," the guy said as he marched out of The Zonderling.

Up on the twelfth floor, Heather ran into Emily and Jennifer. Emily had finally completed the NYFU training after she managed to maintain a scowl when Jennifer played the video of the sneezing panda. It took eight attempts until Emily was able to watch the whole thing without smiling.

"Hey, Heather!" Emily said. "We're going to dinner. Want to join us?"

"No thanks. I got a sandwich on the way home."

Jennifer's phone beeped with a new text message. "My boyfriend is such an idiot," she said as she looked at her phone. "He was supposed to meet me in the parlor after dinner, but he thought he'd be clever and try to sneak in early."

"That guy is your boyfriend? The General caught him!" Heather said. "He had an Altruistic Army uniform and everything."

Jennifer shook her head. "It's not a real uniform. He's a teacher, and he borrowed it from the theater department. It's a Christmas nutcracker costume. Thought he was being so smart. What a dummy."

"The General banned him for a month."

"All talk. If you're a guy who is 'banned' from The Zonderling parlor, all you have to do is put on a baseball hat. They never match you to your photo." Jennifer put her phone back into her pocket. "Let's get going. I'm starving."

"Heather, you could still come down for dessert. The General said that some girls who are students at culinary school set up a pastry table for practice," Emily said.

"Only three people got sick last time," Jennifer said. "Though no one got sick the *first* time." She thought about the last time the culinary school girls had baked pastries. Specifically she thought about the lawn chair that Normal Lisa dragged into the bathroom because the walk from her room to the toilet was too long to reach the safety of the vomitorium. Loretta made a big stink about Normal Lisa "taking over" the bathroom, until Normal Lisa threatened to projectile vomit on Loretta if she said one more word. Loretta backed down in a brief moral victory for the normal residents. "Regardless, those girls can flambé the crap out of a crepe."

"No thanks, guys. I'm beat."

Emily wanted to show Jennifer what she'd learned about the NYFU, so she turned to Heather with a straight face and took a deep breath. "Join us for dinner and potentially poisonous pastries! You need food because you're too skinny!" Emily said aggressively. "And I like your dress, so I hope you don't spill on it!"

"No," Heather said. "I'm going to go to bed. See you later."

As Heather quickly disappeared into her room, Emily proudly turned to Jennifer and said, "I really felt the NYFU!"

"Well, you didn't smile, so points for that. But even in New York, you don't scream at someone to invite them to dinner," Jennifer said. "Unless you're from Staten Island."

Freshly showered and in her pajamas, Heather felt a million times better after washing the daily coating of New York grime down the drain. She couldn't believe the amount of dirt on her face, in her eyes, and in the tissue when she blew her nose. *Where did all of this disgusting black stuff come from?* Heather suspected a lot of it came from choking on bus dust while waiting to cross the street. Bus dust—the grime kicked up by buses when they pull away from a stop—was the great leveler in New York City. No matter how rich someone was, everyone choked on bus dust if they stood on the sidewalk.

Heather grabbed a hair dryer from her closet so she could use it in the bathroom per The Zonderling guidelines. As she turned the doorknob, she heard shuffling feet in the hallway. She looked out of the peephole and saw Benjamin Button slowly moving down the hall in a threadbare adult onesie. *No way.*

Trying to avoid any interaction, Heather looked around her room for an outlet. The outlets were all two-pronged, which luckily fit the hair dryer. She wasn't sure how she was going to use her three-pronged power strip in the retro electrical situation, but that was a problem for another day. She plugged in the dryer and turned it on. Seconds later, the power went out.

Noooooooooooo!

Heather stood in the darkness. Well, Manhattan darkness that was lit by a million streetlights. She sat on her bed for a minute, willing the power back to life. It didn't work.

Suddenly a bullhorn crackled to life in the hallway. "Gentleman on floor!" The General always announced himself this way every time that he entered the residential areas. After all, he was one of the only men allowed on the residential floors. He lived on The Zonderling's top floor, along with other Altruistic Army personnel like Captain David and Lieutenant Rachel.

"Attention residents!" The General said. "There's a mandatory meeting about contraband electrical items in the cafetorium. It begins in five minutes."

Heather heard the stairway door close as The General walked down to a new floor. "Gentleman on floor! Attention residents!"

All traces of dinner had been cleared from the cafetorium, but the lingering smell of salmon en croute hung in the humid August air. Residents sat at the dining tables as they waited for the meeting to begin. Wearing street clothes and a Crappie Lodge and Resort baseball hat, Heather tried to make sure that no one could see her damp hair.

The General stood on stage with a flashlight and pleaded with the residents. "Please, someone confess. No one wants another court-martial like when we found an empty wine bottle in the ninth-floor garbage."

On paper The Zonderling was alcohol-free. In reality the smart girls just dumped their empty booze bottles in the garbage on the corner of New Holland Circle and Limburg Street. Some resident had to have been super lazy to just toss the bottle in the shared bathroom trash. The court-martial about the ninth-floor wine bottle lasted two days until Loretta magically produced evidence that implicated her nemesis, Martha. The General sentenced Martha to one day of KP duty, but Martha managed to pawn this off on an unsuspecting English-as-a-second-language resident who didn't question the old lady's instructions to clean grease traps.

No one responded to The General's question about who was responsible for the blackout. The residents sat silently in the dark room, their faces lit by the glow of smartphones as they posted about the power outage, *Beauty Queen Dial-Up*, and the heat wave. Most residents were primarily concerned with getting power back to recharge their devices.

The General looked around the quiet room and took a deep breath. "No one has anything to tell me? Don't make me cancel the Floradora Flip Social."

The Floradora Flip Social was a beloved tradition that started when residents said good-bye to General Charlie Van Der Zonderling when he retired to the sunny beaches of Florida. One of the Altruistic Army lieutenants found the recipe for the icy nonalcoholic Floradora Flip and thought it would be a more fitting send-off to Florida than the suggested ice cream social since the name sounded like Florida. The Floradora Flip Social was such a hit that it became an annual tradition in honor of General Van Der Zonderling.

"The social is before movie night this week," The General said. "I'll cancel it, I really will."

"The hell you will!" Loretta yelled.

"Language!" Porn Lisa said.

"You can't cancel tradition!" Helen added. "It's not fair!"

Other long-term residents began yelling about the absolute right to have their annual Floradora Flip. Younger residents were totally cool if they missed out on drinks made with powdered milk, bananas, lemon juice, and molasses.

"No, it's not fair," The General said, trying to calm the crowd. "But is it fair that I'm missing the new documentary about pens that's airing right now? My TV went black when they were just getting to the revolutionary change from fountain pens to ballpoint." He waited a beat, hoping that he had been able to successfully guilt someone into confessing. He hadn't—most people didn't share his love of pens because most people only cared about whether the pen worked. It was time for The General to deploy the bomb.

"OK, ladies. Unless someone confesses, or Captain David can fix the lights in the next few minutes, you leave me with no choice," The General took a deep breath before continuing, hoping someone would confess before he had to finish his final thought—nope. "I'm going to have to lock the TV room during the next episode of *Beauty Queen Dial-Up.*"

The cafetorium erupted with absolute fury as if the Floradora Flip Social had been canceled forever. Loretta stood up and screamed, "Don't you dare! I have plans to watch that show!"

"Then someone better confess, gosh darn it! The new episode is going to be good too," The General said. While watching the documentary *Ballpoint: The Best Point*, he had seen a new promo for *Beauty Queen Dial-Up*. The clips promised a hilarious new show in which the five beauty queens were desperately hitting a desktop computer with a doll, a keyboard, a fishing rod, a potted plant, and a bow-and-arrow set.

"They get downgraded to a twenty-eight-point-eight modem," The General told the residents. He chuckled thinking about Miss Teen Vermont screaming, "Just tell us who wore it best!"

Loretta was not about to let anyone come between her and *Beauty Queen Dial-Up*. She immediately pointed at seventy-three-year-old Martha and said, "Martha was using a mug warmer. That's what zapped the power."

"It's true!" Helen said. "I saw her!" Helen was always a loyal crony to Loretta about 99 percent of the time. The 1 percent disloyalty came from the fact that Helen secretly admired Martha's snazzy knit scarves. In fact, Helen was such a fan of Martha's scarves that she bought an identical one that she wore only once she was out of view of The Zonderling.

Loretta was confident that the mug warmer accusation was a good one. She knew mug warmers could zap the power because she'd done it several times in the past. Loretta had recently been publicly blaming Martha for power issues, cleanliness issues, and basically anything that bothered her.

It all started when Loretta decided that she had outgrown the room that she had been in since the Watergate scandal. Loretta had moved to The Zonderling after a divorce because she wanted to show her no-good ex that she most certainly *could* stay in the city without moving in with her son. She'd been at The Zonderling for so long that she either needed more space or a storage unit, or she needed to start throwing things out. But Loretta knew that throwing things out was always a big mistake—someday she would definitely need that gigantic plastic bag of plastic bags.

Corner rooms were the most valuable at The Zonderling because they were the biggest. They also had two windows, which meant cooler summers and more light. And since no one was allowed to own a mini fridge, it also meant twice as much space for storing perishable food on the windowsill during the cold winters.

After the former corner room resident moved out, citing recent loud noise from Loretta's fire alarm, The General selected Martha from the handful of room applicants that included Loretta. From that moment, Martha became Loretta's nemesis, and Martha was now known in management for her (false) reckless behavior, which made her the perfect patsy for all of Loretta's crimes. Or even crimes of unknown origin, like the current blackout.

"Lies!" Martha screamed. Heather sank into her seat with guilt as Martha continued. "It's not true! How would they even know what I'm doing in my room anyway? And this is the first time I've even seen Loretta or Helen today!"

"Oh my. Her sight is going with her memory. Her TV time should be signed over to me," Loretta said patronizingly.

"Definitely," Helen said.

"You're just framing me because I beat you to the TV room today and you couldn't watch that talk show you like, *Celebrity Yada Yada Yada*," Martha said.

"Prove it!" Loretta yelled. "You watch enough *Military Police: Texas!*"

Loretta hated police procedurals, so she squatted in the TV room any time that *Military Police: Texas* was on TV, just to spite Martha. It didn't matter what Loretta had to watch, so long as Martha couldn't watch *Military Police: Texas*. This proved more difficult than Loretta imagined because, like most procedurals, *Military Police: Texas* aired in constant syndication. It was frequently on in the afternoon, which conflicted with church bingo, and Loretta never missed church bingo.

"Military investigations, great show!" The General said to anyone who cared, which was nearly all of the older ladies. *Military Police: Texas* was the new *Monk*, which was the new *Matlock*.

"I know you stole my walker the other day, Loretta!" Martha said.

"See, she's delusional!" Loretta yelled. "Her walker's sitting right next to her!"

"Because The General found it by the bathroom. You should be ashamed!"

"*I* should be ashamed? *You* should be ashamed!" Loretta yelled. "You only use that thing to guilt people into a seat on the subway. It's absolutely outrageous, just like the messes you make in the bathroom!"

"Enough!" The General said. "Martha, you've been warned in the past about mug warmers. I can't believe you're still using one."

"But I don't own a mug—"

"Three weeks of KP duty."

"That's not fair!" Martha said.

"It *is* unfair, Martha," Loretta said. "You should have at least six weeks of KP."

The General sighed, exasperated. "No one should even have a mug warmer, as per page forty-two, item three, paragraph one of The Zonderling Code of Conduct."

The lights flickered back to life, and everyone cheered for Captain David's handy Kennedy-era electrical skills that were required for fixing anything at The Zonderling. Luckily he was an expert at Kennedy-era electricity because he acquired the knowledge firsthand during the Kennedy era.

Residents headed back to their rooms, especially Heather, who scuttled away as fast as she could before anyone could ask her about the wet hat on her head. Unfortunately nothing got past Jennifer, who immediately noticed Heather's damp hat, and followed behind to get to the bottom of it.

With the lights on, The General spotted Emily in the crowd and ran up to her. "Miss Benson! All of that talk about *Military Police: Texas* reminds me about something I wanted to tell you since you also love movies."

"Oh for fun! What's up?"

"For our upcoming movie night at The Zonderling, I scheduled my favorite military moving picture show!"

"*Private Benjamin?*"

"I do love that one," The General said. "OK, I've scheduled my second-favorite military moving picture show— *Pearl Harbor!*"

Emily squealed at such a high pitch it reminded The General of the time Miss Beauty Queen Idaho thought she stumbled across a Wi-Fi signal in the shower during the *Beauty Queen Dial-Up* premiere.

"General!" Emily shouted. "I'm in that movie!"

"No!" The General was *very* impressed.

"We were in Hawaii for my aunt's fourth wedding. I was an extra! I met Josh Hartnett's stunt double!"

"Well, if this isn't the most exciting thing at The Zonderling since K. Johnston!"

Tired and pissed off, Jennifer confronted Heather in the twelfth-floor hallway.

"Bathroom notes are there for a reason," Jennifer said.

"I don't," Heather stuttered. "I don't know what—"

Jennifer took a step toward Heather. "A tiny little mug warmer can no longer zap the electricity in the building. Not after Captain David upgraded the building from a fuse box to a 1963 circuit breaker last month."

For a moment Heather didn't say anything. Then she was immediately overcome with a case of verbal diarrhea. "Please don't say anything! I don't have street skills! Where would I go?" she babbled. "I'd have to move in with the Dick. The Dick is the only person I know. My only option is the Dick!"

Hearing the commotion, Emily excitedly opened her door. "Are we role-playing New Yorkers?" She began prepping like the actress she wanted to be. "NYFU. NYFU. FUNY!" Emily said to herself. "Ha-ha! *FUNY* is like *funny!*"

"Look, Heather, I know you probably had a crappy day at the bank, or someone spit on you when you walked down the street, and I'm sorry," Jennifer said. "But I have to be at work soon. If you kill the power again—and therefore the fans—I will destroy you."

Jennifer walked away, leaving Emily and Heather in the hall. Emily, now having properly prepped her NYFU face, targeted Heather. In an over-the-top voice, Emily yelled, "Free stress test? Are you saying I have aliens in my brain?"

"What are you talking about?" Heather asked.

"I don't need a stress test! *You* need a stress test!" As Emily ranted about aliens, she backed Heather into the bathroom.

"Emily! Stop it!" Heather said, worried that Jennifer would return because of the noise. "People are trying to sleep."

Emily snapped out of her NYFU face and smiled. "Oh man, I think I finally did it! You seemed rattled!"

"No kidding! You're yelling at me!"

"Cool! I was practicing my NYFU face. Jennifer said that I needed to have one so that people don't try to con me. Or sit next to me on the subway. Or ask me for directions."

"I think you've got it."

"Awesome!" Emily said. "Hi, Loretta!"

Loretta hadn't seen the girls when she entered the bathroom and was startled to find someone else in there. She quickly became angry. "What are you doing in here?"

"Chatting," Emily said.

"It's quiet hours. You are violating quiet hours with your talking!" Loretta said at a level that most certainly also violated quiet hours.

"You're the one yelling," Heather said.

"You shouldn't be talking in here! You can expect a noise complaint to be filed with The General tomorrow."

"Jeez, fine. We'll go," Heather said. "Enjoy using the toilet in complete silence."

As Loretta argued with Heather and Emily, Jennifer walked past Loretta's room, the door of which was uncharacteristically ajar.

She left it open! Jennifer thought. *She never leaves it open!* Jennifer inched closer. Keeping enough distance to claim she wasn't snooping, she peered into the dark room and saw floor-to-ceiling piles of the wrenches that Emily mentioned. Before she could get her phone out of her pocket to take a photo of the evidence for The General, a familiar voice yelled at her.

"What are you doing?" Loretta snapped.

Dammit!

Jennifer whirled around and stared at Loretta. "Walking to my room."

"Why is my room open?" Loretta pushed past her and grabbed the doorknob, pulling the door shut. "What did you take?"

"I didn't take anything. God, Loretta! Paranoid much?"

"You broke into my room."

"No, I didn't. The breeze from your window probably blew open the door because you didn't lock it."

"Stay away from my stuff," Loretta sneered.

"No problem." Jennifer started to walk away but then turned around. With a forced smile that was the ultimate passive-aggressive Minnesota version of the NYFU face, Jennifer decided to kill Loretta with kindness. "Have a great night, Loretta!"

"You take that back!"

"Bye, Loretta! Sleep tight!"

Heather sat on her bed, in the dark, wondering what she was doing. Nothing was going right. She couldn't even dry her hair in privacy without killing the power for an entire building. She also really wanted a glass of milk, but she couldn't have one because she didn't have a refrigerator. And the thought of returning to the NRI tomorrow gave her knots in her stomach. Mira was the only normal person at International Bank.

The city lights were so bright that it took forever to fall asleep. Heather opened the nightstand drawer to get her sleeping mask. When she tried to shut the drawer, it wouldn't close because something was jammed at the back. She removed the drawer and reached back to remove the object. It was a wadded up piece of paper that said, "Cindy, stop playing that loud music! I can't hear the radio updates about OJ. I will report you to The General. AGAIN!" It was signed *Loretta*.

Heather crumpled it up and threw it into the trash. Then she took a deep breath, put on the sleeping mask, and tried to think happy thoughts about Nick spilling coffee on Vikram's stupid Italian shoes.

FOURTEEN

The next day around noon, Jennifer saw Loretta and Emily exit The Zonderling together. Emily was carrying two large garbage bags, one of which she heaved into the pile of trash on the corner of New Holland Circle and Limburg Street. Then Loretta grabbed the other bag and dragged it down the road. Emily waved good-bye in vain and sat on the stoop to look at her phone.

Jennifer approached The Zonderling. "Hey, Emily."

"Hiya! What a gorgeous day, hey?"

"I think we're upwind from the melting garbage today," Jennifer said.

"Guess what?" Emily said. "I just got a callback for a job!"

"You got a callback already? That's amazing! For what?"

"The Urban Woodsman Workshop!"

"Oh, so, like it's..."

"On Broadway!"

"Yes, but it's a store."

"In the heart of the theater district!"

"So you can just say interview instead of callback."

"It would be so cool to work on Broadway."

"You're definitely going to need your NYFU face to survive in Times Square. Good luck," Jennifer said. She pointed at Loretta's garbage that Emily had carried to the curb. "What's the deal with that? Why are you still helping Loretta dump her trash out here?"

"I'm so bad at thinking of excuses. It was easier to just carry it out."

Jennifer pointed in the direction that Loretta had walked. "Why is she carrying a bag with her?"

"That's the church donation. She always has one for the trash and one for church donation."

"What on earth does Loretta have that anyone would want?"

"I don't know," Emily said. "Both bags have the same lumpy things because it never matters which one goes in the trash."

"Why don't both go to church?"

"She said one was plenty for church. And then she told me to mind my own business."

Jennifer stared at the bag. "Let's open it."

"Eww, I don't want to look at her garbage."

"Then I'll open it." Jennifer walked over to the garbage pile and gashed a hole in Loretta's bag with her room key. "Oh my God!"

"What is it?"

"Come over and look."

"I don't want to look."

"It's not gross. It's just more proof that Loretta is the worst."

"You promise?"

"I promise, it's fine. I'm more worried about what she's up to than what she put in here."

Emily timidly looked in the garbage bag that Jennifer held open. "Well, jeez, what the..."

"...hell Granny Panties?" Nick said as he dropped a package on Heather's desk. He frantically swigged from an energy drink while hovering between Heather and Mira. Nick always made sure he took full advantage of the energy drinks, which meant filling his backpack each evening to share the wealth with his roommates who foolishly slaved away in dumb jobs where the only free thing they got at work was tap water.

"Huh?" Heather said. She was so miserable and tired from the late-night cafetorium meeting that even two double espressos hadn't helped her alertness level.

"I thought you were quote, unquote, *responsible*," he said as he took another swig. "Are you trying to annoy me like when my GF makes me go to baby showers at bars? Because it's still a bar regardless of the dumbass diaper game with melted chocolate that she makes me play." He took another swig from the bottle. "And if she doesn't want me mooning the bartender and singing Elton John, then she shouldn't take me to a baby shower at a bar. That's on her."

Heather rolled her eyes. "Pickup is in five hours, Nick. Go away!"

"Heather, it's a priority overnight. From Vikram. That he sent *yesterday*."

"What?" Heather immediately snapped out of her mood. Her heart raced at the guilt from not doing her job properly. Little did she know that it was Vikram who hadn't done his job properly. Yesterday, while on his way to drop the package in the collection bin, Vikram stopped in the break room to grab an energy drink. While in the break room, he received a text from his buddy on the foreign exchange team about free tickets to a polo match hosted by Très Chic Champagne, Di Moda Italiano Cars, and the prince of an obscure European country mainly known for its status as a tax haven. The idea of discussing luxury watches and hedge funds with minor royalty was enough to distract Vikram, who left the package sitting by the refrigerator. Nick found it the next day when he chugged his morning energy drink.

Heather grabbed the package from Nick and leaped out of her chair.

"I don't know why you're running, Granny Panties! It was supposed to arrive an hour ago." Nick subconsciously turned his wrist to check his watch and forgot that he was holding a drink with the same hand—a drink that was now spilled all over Mira's expensive jeans.

"Nick!" Mira yelled. She held out her hand. "Thirty bucks."

This demand for money didn't surprise Nick because she asked for thirty dollars every time he accidentally spilled something on her, which was quite often given how jittery he got after a few energy drinks. He always paid Mira the money he owed, because Mira didn't mess around. She once told him that if he didn't pay for her dry cleaning, she would no longer remind him of his girlfriend's birthday, her favorite food, or her mom's name.

Nick took out his wallet and gave her thirty dollars. "Sorry," he said.

"This should be it. We're directly below Loretta's room," Jennifer said as she stared at the ceiling.

"I wonder if there's an eleventh-floor version of Loretta," Emily said. Both Emily and Jennifer were carrying two large bottles of water as they looked around the floor beneath theirs.

"There's only one Loretta," Jennifer said. "But there was a girl who obsessively turned off the bathroom lights to save energy, even if people were inside. She moved out last year when she married the heir to a lumber fortune. Met him on the subway."

"Wow! That's crazy!"

"I know, I can't believe she talked to someone on the subway." Jennifer opened a bottle of water. "I guess I should pour the water as close as I can to the door to make it look like it leaked from Loretta's room."

"Are you sure we should do this?" Emily was nervous. One time she participated in a squirt gun fight on her dorm floor. It did not end well after she accidentally soaked the dean's favorite bison head mount in the lounge.

"This place has been around forever. I don't think it's possible to damage anything at The Zonderling. Besides, we both know there's something really sketchy going on in her room."

"The General was pretty concerned about her accumulating any wrenches."

"And she has cockroaches."

"Gross, I forgot about that."

"Whatever is happening in there, her room is a fire hazard. This is the only way to get to the bottom of it." Jennifer poured one bottle of water on the floor. As she opened another bottle, she looked at Emily who was chugging one of her two bottles. "Stop wasting the water!"

"It's so hot," Emily protested. "And this is so cold!"

"Pour it on the floor."

Emily took one last gulp before dumping both bottles of water on the carpet. Jennifer took her last bottle and threw water toward the ceiling.

"That looks so real!" Emily said as she looked up.

Jennifer took a picture of the wet floor and ceiling. "All set. Let's go down and show this photo to The General.

Then we'll fill out a work order about the water leak in Loretta's room."

Heather paused on the sidewalk to catch her breath. She couldn't believe she had actually pushed someone out of the way because he was walking too slowly, but he was way taller so he had no excuse for not using his long legs. Heather looked at the street sign—only three blocks from the shipping store. She was hoping to charm the teenage employees into accepting the package for some sort of crazy rush delivery. As she gulped for air, she read the recipient's address. Then she looked at the building across the street. *For Pete's sake! What a freaking lazy moron!*

The General, Captain David, Jennifer, and Emily hurried to Loretta's room on the twelfth floor.

"I don't know what's going on in her room, General, but that was a big leak down on eleven," Jennifer said.

"Thank you for reporting it immediately," The General said. "Good thing we have Captain David, who can fix anything. Assuming that Loretta isn't barricading her door this time."

The General knocked. "Excuse me, Loretta? It's The General. We have a water situation on eleven. Can we have a quick look in your room?" There was no response, so The

General knocked again. "Loretta? It's me. The General. Of The Zonderling."

Jennifer worried about The General getting bogged down with unnecessary politeness, so she intervened. "We saw her leave the building a few minutes ago. I don't think she's here."

The General looked at Captain David. "Should we go in?"

"It's a water leak, sir. Remember the dumbwaiter flood of 2006? We need to contain this right away."

"I concur." The General took out his key and opened the door. As soon as he saw inside, he said the only thing he could think of: "Oyster crackers!"

FIFTEEN

Back at her desk, Heather tuned out the world. Thank goodness for her noise-canceling headphones that her mom gave her for graduation. Her feet were sore from running in heels, so she had changed back into her commuting sneakers. She no longer cared about trying to look like a magazine photo. Her makeup melted off of her face within seconds of standing on the sweltering subway platform anyway. Combining that with sweat stains and humidity-soaked hair, she didn't know how anyone ever managed to look like a fashion magazine photo—she was starting to suspect that those magazine pictures were majorly staged.

Heather robotically punched the keyboard and glared at Nick's head, wishing that her eyes were capable of shooting lasers. Suddenly Vikram swooped in and perched on her desk nearly knocking over her cup of coffee. She slowly pulled the headphones down around her neck in order to listen to his rant.

"Hey, temp!" Vikram said. "My package was supposed to be delivered already, but the tracking number says it wasn't even picked up! What the hell happened?"

"My name is *Heather*."

"Well, *Heather*? What happened?"

"It wasn't picked up," Heather said. "I literally put it into the hands of your client. You shipped it across the street. I can see the building right there!" She pointed to it through the window.

"What's wrong with you?" Vikram yelled. "Knowing where it is at all times is the most exciting part of shipping with a tracking number!"

Vikram loved tracking numbers. He spent a significant portion of his day refreshing the tracking number website for the instant gratification of keeping tabs on his packages. When they were delivered, it sometimes felt like a letdown because the thrill of the game was over. There were many things that Vikram loved about tracking numbers.

He liked the excitement of when his package went somewhere unexpected. "Cheating on JFK with Newark. Naughty, naughty!"

He pleaded like a jilted lover when a package was somewhere he knew that it shouldn't be. "Stuck in customs? You're domestic. Who are you seeing in customs, you bitch?"

He tingled with anticipation when the status was labeled *out for delivery*. "Out for delivery," he cooed yesterday as he looked at his phone. "You got a package for me? You got a pack—wait. No, that's not right." He turned to Mira. "*It* doesn't have a package. *I* have the package. A *big* package."

"Yeah, yeah, we get it. No one cares." Mira rolled her eyes. "Have you approved any of our purchase orders today?"

He would thrust his hands into the air with exhilaration when the package was finally delivered and yell, "Signature confirmation! We have signature confirmation!" Then he'd high-five Nick, who was so slick that he could high-five anyone midwalk without breaking stride.

"Um, OK," Heather said. "But I thought it was weird—"

"Who gave you authority to think? Nick, did you authorize thinking?"

"Bro, you know the only woman that I've authorized to think is my cleaning lady. And that's for obvious reasons related to my party on National Stick Something in Honey Day," Nick replied.

"Oh yeah, National Stick Something in Honey Day!" Vikram and Nick high-fived.

"You know what? I forgot to send your package yesterday because I *wasn't thinking!*" Heather said as she stood up. It would have looked more awesome if she didn't have to quickly grab her desk to steady herself. Somehow one of her shoelaces got wrapped around the chair wheel, but she wasn't going to let on that she was tethered to her chair. Heather made it look like she had very dramatically placed her hands on her desk, like someone with something very dramatic to say. Luckily, she did.

"But I *was* thinking when I corrected the mistake, because I could walk your priority overnight package to its destination. I don't understand why you were shipping it anyway," Heather said. "Why were you spending the money? So it could spend an evening at JFK shagging a British package? Or having a *ménage à trois* with two French packages? I don't really understand what you think boxes do when you're not watching."

Vikram shrugged.

"But oh no! There was no tracking number! Excuse me! I thought banks liked saving money. Don't you want to tell your boss that you saved money?" Heather said. And since she was fired up, she added, "By the way, *I* don't have an accent. *I* sound like the news. Just because I'm from a flyover state doesn't mean that I milked cows every day. That was just on school field trips!"

"Sure. 'Field trips,'" Nick said, gesturing with air quotes.

"*Why?*" Heather yelled as she turned to Nick. "*Why are you here?*"

After a long, awkward beat, Vikram burst out laughing. "Ha-ha! Save money! That's a good one, Heather! We don't need to save money. We're a bank. We get bailouts."

Vikram's Bluetooth flashed. "Go for Vik. No, honey, I don't know what my son did." Vikram rolled his eyes and made a big show of miming shooting himself in his head because his wife was *so* annoying. "What? *Expelled!* Third strike? No son of mine is going to public school in Jersey!"

Vikram stormed off down the hall to deal with the prospect that his days of shoulder rubbing with the elite parents at Upper Crustington Academy might end if his oldest son, Logan, got expelled. Apparently Logan had been toilet-papering houses in an affluent New Jersey neighborhood, one of which happened to be the home of the Upper Crustington vice principal, who was not amused.

Heather sat down and unhooked her shoelace from the chair wheel.

Nick looked at her and said, "Wow! You have bigger balls than I thought."

"Thanks." Heather couldn't believe her ears. "That's very nice of you to say. You know when I first realized we were working together—"

"I'm totally impressed. For real, Granny Panties."

And there it is. "My name is Heather, Nick. *Heather!*"

"Duh. I've only known you for like, my whole life."

"Then you should know that it is not OK to call me Granny Panties. It never was OK to call me Granny Panties."

"Lighten up!"

"And it's certainly not appropriate now! We're adults, we're coworkers, and there's an HR department at extension five-five-five-five."

"Jeez, fine, I won't call you Granny Panties."

"Thank you!"

"OK? God, relax, GP."

"Ugh! Nick! Come on!"

"Baby steps, Heather," Mira said. "Baby steps. Or the poor boy's head will explode."

It had been a very successful day for Loretta at Our Savior's Divine Blessed Sorrow of the Super Sad Sacred Heart Church. As she rode the elevator back to the twelfth floor of The Zonderling, she counted her bingo winnings. *Nearly seven hundred dollars with zero buy-in money. Not bad,* thought Loretta.

The only downside to the day had been when Joyce, a very competitive ninety-four-year-old woman, attacked Loretta with a red bingo marker. To be fair, Loretta did mark some false numbers on Joyce's cards, but that was only because Joyce took the last piece of coffee cake. A yelling match started when Joyce figured out what Loretta had done. The screaming and allegations ended when Father Patrick broke up the fight and escorted Joyce out of the fellowship hall after she drew the large red line on Loretta's forearm.

Loretta was trying to clean the marker ink with spit as she walked down the hall, which was why she didn't immediately notice Captain David and Emily in front of her room.

"Voldemort!" Emily yelled in a panic. "Voldemort has landed!"

"What are you all doing?" Loretta snapped. "Why is my door open?"

"Water was leaking from your room down to the eleventh floor," Captain David said. "We had to enter your room to fix it."

"That's a load of bull!" Loretta said as she charged past Captain David and saw The General and Jennifer in her room. "Get out of here immediately!"

"Loretta, I'm rarely at a loss for words," The General said. "But...oyster crackers, Loretta."

"You always complain about the bathroom and the toilets," Jennifer said. "But how can the bathroom ever be OK when you're stealing all of the toilet paper!" She pointed to three garbage bags bursting with the stolen goods.

"I *bought* that! The Zonderling can't even keep the bathrooms stocked," Loretta said. "It's appalling that—"

"You didn't buy those. After you alerted me to the bathroom problems during the residents' meeting, I began marking all stock," The General said. He picked up a roll and showed it to Loretta. "See? Inside the roll there's a big blue Z. I got the idea from a documentary about the original *Ocean's 11.*"

"That doesn't prove anything!" Loretta said. "Looks like an N to me anyway."

"Speaking from an electrical safety standpoint, I have to say that the multiple mug warmers in your room are problematic," Captain David said.

"You always complain about response time on pest control, but this might be ground zero, Loretta," The General said. "That stack of dirty dishes you took from the dining room is a violation of section five, paragraph three, line eleven." In all of his years at The Zonderling, The General had never seen a room situation quite like Loretta's. He was most annoyed by the massive pile of stolen remotes (mixed with a handful of wrenches) from the TV room. Loretta had apparently been stealing the remotes for years in an effort to maintain control of the shared TV. When she was bored, Loretta also used the remotes as a weapon of chaos against unsuspecting residents who had TVs in their rooms.

Several decades of fashion magazines sat next to the pile of remotes. This was arguably the most puzzling find in the room, unless Loretta used the worst-dressed columns as daily inspiration. Jennifer and Emily had several theories about the magazines such as Loretta cutting them up for the ransom-style notes in the bathroom, stacking them to be tables, and using them to smash cockroaches.

"All of these dishes and remotes. And wrenches, Loretta? *Wrenches?* We talked about this!" The General said as he picked up a wrench from the remote pile.

"I own that wrench!"

"No, you don't." The General turned the wrench over in his hand to reveal a stamp. The stamp said *Return to Captain David*, which The General promptly did.

"Thank you, General," Captain David said.

"Stealing from The Zonderling is a serious offense, Loretta."

"This entire room is a serious offense!" Jennifer said. "I knew it would be." She thanked her lucky stars that Loretta's room was the hoarding fire hazard that she suspected. The stolen property in the room was a nice bonus.

"You can't be in here. I have rights," Loretta said. "I'm an American. And this search and seizure is definitely against the Constitution."

"But it's not against page thirty-four, paragraph eighteen of The Zonderling Code of Conduct," The General said. "Written by General Van Der Zonderling *himself*."

Sixteen

Heather had just returned to The Zonderling and was standing at the bathroom sink trying to clean a mayonnaise stain from her skirt. "Heather!" Emily squealed as she walked into the bathroom. "You're finally back from work. Guess what? I got a job!"

"Congratulations!"

"It's at the Urban Woodsman Workshop in *Times Square!*"

"You're working in Times Square? I'm so jealous!"

"I know! Jennifer was like, 'I'd slit my wrists if I had to work in Times Square.' But I'm like—"

"It's in the middle of everything!"

"Exactly! You get it. I don't know why she hates Times Square so much," Emily said. "Anyway, there's a bar in the Urban Woodsman Workshop and I'm going to be one of the lady lumberjack servers. They were really impressed with my demo reel of snowmobile commercials. They said I was perfect lady lumberjack material."

The bar manager of the Urban Woodsman Workshop had definitely been excited by Emily's demo reel. Most of the stacked girls that he hired were bridge and tunnel, but Emily had actually grown up near some sort of actual forest situation where there had probably been real lumberjacks. Plus, if the store ever installed a bucking-bronco-type snowmobile ride, Emily would be the perfect poster girl. She was definitely lady lumberjack material.

The Urban Woodsman Workshop was as close to a lumber store as one would ever find in Manhattan. It had a working woodshop that appealed to hipster Paul Bunyan wannabes who didn't understand what *two-by-four* actually meant so they called all wood *two-by-four*. The store also sold a bunch of expensive wooden toys that kids didn't want but moms loved because they were handcrafted on organic farms upstate. The toy manager called it "farm to playroom." But most important, the Urban Woodsman Workshop appealed to every horny teenager and finance bro who wandered past the store. If they looked in the large, well-lit window, they'd see a team of sexy lady lumberjacks serving craft beer in the bar.

"I start my lumberjack training tomorrow," Emily said.

"That's awesome," Heather said. "Meet you in the cafetorium for dinner?"

"See you there!"

Heather walked into the hall as The General threw open the stairwell door. "Gentleman on floor!" He leaned over and put his hands on his knees in order to catch his breath. "Heather! Have you seen a laundry cart?"

"No."

"Are you sure? This laundry cart I'm looking for," he panted. "It's big. It's made of canvas. It has a boy hiding inside of it."

"Nope. Haven't seen any laundry carts."

"No? Oyster crackers!" He barreled back into the stairwell and ran down to the eleventh floor. "Gentleman on floor!"

Heather continued down the hall and saw Jennifer. "I'm so glad I ran into you," Heather said. "I'm really sorry about the hair dryer last night, and messing up the power."

"Oh my gosh, it's OK. I was just in a bad mood and took it out on you."

"You've been so nice to me with advice and everything. I hope—"

"Water under the bridge. Heather, you're never going to believe what happened today! We finally got Loretta!" Jennifer told Heather about everything that had happened that afternoon, starting with the staged water leak. "You know how she never opened her door, but it looked like her room was piled with crap?"

"Just from what I've overheard. I've never actually seen inside."

"It was even worse than any of us thought. It was like she was auditioning for a hoarding reality show."

"Yikes!"

"Look at the pictures."

Heather grabbed Jennifer's phone. "Is all of that toilet paper?"

"Yes! Loretta was stealing it from the bathroom!"

"Why?"

"Who knows? She wouldn't say," Jennifer said. "She's just been throwing some of it on the curb via Emily and then donating the rest to the church down the road."

"Is that a thing in New York? I didn't know that churches wanted toilet paper donations."

"Apparently Our Savior's Divine Blessed Sorrow of the Super Sad Sacred Heart did."

Heather swiped through some more photos. "That wall looks like something out of a serial killer's basement on *Military Police: Texas*."

"Because it's covered with clippings from the OJ Simpson trial."

"Oh my gosh!" Emily said as she emerged from the bathroom. "Are you showing her the photos?"

"Yeah!"

"It was nuts," Emily said to Heather.

"Loretta's been staring at that OJ craziness since 1995," Jennifer swiped to another photo. "Look at this one. She had prewritten angry bathroom notes. Who does that?"

"After The General went inside her room, how did you explain the water leak ruse?"

"That's the best part!"

Much to Jennifer's delight, something was actually leaking all over the floor in Loretta's room—a large duct-taped humidifier. It wasn't enough water to leak down to the next floor, but there was so much going on in Loretta's room that no one thought too much about the logistics. It was also beyond comprehension as to why anyone would want to use a humidifier in August, especially in a building without air conditioning. Loretta liked swimming in humidity, a nasty situation that explained the large amount of black mold growing in her room. Apparently her enthusiasm for spraying mold cleaner didn't extend beyond the walls of the bathroom.

After a quick meeting between The General and Captain David, they decided that Loretta would be much better off at the Altruistic Army's senior residence, Linden Tower, effective immediately. Loretta was furious about the move because she was losing her alpha position at The Zonderling—instead she was going to be the *new* resident. Loretta's son, Larry, offered a room to his mom, but she wouldn't hear of it because he had a new girlfriend (named Katniss), and she didn't want to interfere with any chance of her son finally getting married. Loretta figured she could move in whenever Larry and Katniss tied the knot, and then she could show them how to properly run a household.

The Zonderling residents were overjoyed. Nothing made Jennifer happier than thinking of Loretta moving into a building filled with a bunch of other bossy, established Lorettas. However, Loretta's departure from SoDeDyFa bummed out two very different people: Father Patrick from Our Savior's Divine Blessed Sorrow of the Super Sad Sacred Heart, and Vikram's oldest son, Logan. Turns out that Loretta ran a scheme where she stole the toilet paper from The Zonderling and traded it for bingo cards at Our Savior's Divine Blessed Sorrow of the Super Sad Sacred Heart. Father Patrick was more than happy to trade bingo cards for the luxurious two-ply toilet paper—he could finally stop fielding complaints about the scratchy one-ply that the church normally stocked in the bathrooms. Loretta stole more toilet paper than she could carry to the church, mainly because she wanted to punish The Zonderling residents, "who didn't deserve it." The extra toilet paper that she couldn't carry to the church ended up on the street where Logan discovered it on his way home from school.

Logan, blessed with the same entrepreneurial skills of his dad, took the toilet paper from the garbage and brought it back home to New Jersey. He told his dad that the additional bags were full of months of dirty gym clothes. When Logan got to New Jersey, he sold the toilet paper to neighborhood kids, who had a great time decorating the surrounding homes. Logan was selling the thick two-ply after all, the kind that hung on branches without ripping. The only house that Logan personally toilet-papered was the home of Vikram's boss, Hugh Fletcher, because the yard had the best trees for holding long white streamers.

Being English, Hugh had zero sense of humor about his home being covered in toilet paper, or *toilet roll* as he called it when he phoned Vikram to complain about seeing Logan in the front yard. As punishment, Vikram had to sign up for five CRAP volunteer activities before the end of the year. Vikram's executive parking privileges were also immediately revoked, which was the most depressing thing that ever happened to Vikram during his career at International Bank. Having his parking privileges revoked was even more depressing than the time he accidentally deleted Sir Julian Frostbite's personal cell number that he overheard Sir Julian give to a secretary.

SEVENTEEN

It was evening at The Zonderling, and Heather was busy pinning some photographs onto the bulletin board in her room. She had purchased a tiny TV with rabbit ears, but she was still trying to find a spot for the antenna where it could pickup the broadcast networks. The strongest signals were for numerous Spanish and Chinese stations, but Heather did manage to get one local English channel. It was the channel she'd seen in the elevator on her first day at International Bank—and the anchor was still talking about the bluefin tuna at SoDeDyFa Sushi. *Sheesh! I always thought that the universal language of local news was impending weather doom, not monster fish.*

Heather heard her phone beep, and she looked at the text from her mom: "Hope your job is OK and you made nice friends! Do you need more cheese curds?" As Heather was about to answer, she heard a knock on her door from Jennifer and Emily.

"Hey, you! Want to join us in the cafetorium for movie night?" Emily said. "And maybe a Floradora Flip?"

"Shoot, I totally forgot about the social," Heather said.

"Trust me, you don't want to drink it anyway," Jennifer said. "It's bananas, molasses, and powdered milk."

"Oh yeah," Emily said. "I keep forgetting that it's not orange juice. It sounds like it should be a fizzy orange juice punch."

"Forget about the Floradora Flip because there is free popcorn and soda," Jennifer said.

"Fun! Thanks for asking me." Heather's phone beeped with another message from her mom as she grabbed her keys: "Is your job near Central Park?" Heather locked her door and answered the text while Emily and Jennifer walked to the elevator.

"I can't wait for you to see me in *Pearl Harbor*. You won't believe it!" Emily said.

"Come on, Heather!" Jennifer said.

"One sec," Heather typed a message to her mom: "Thx, I'm great. No, not near Central Park. Just walk through it to get to work." As she hurried down the hall, she heard a series of beeps from incoming texts and switched her phone to silent.

"Hurry up!" Emily said as she held the elevator doors.

"What's the rush?" Heather said when she stepped into the elevator.

"We want to snag the couch by the window," Jennifer said. "It's closest to the air conditioning and has the fewest unidentifiable stains."

Suddenly the girls heard the loud, shuffling feet of Benjamin Button approaching.

"Emily!" Jennifer said. "Hit the *close* button!"

"Which one?" Emily panicked as she scanned the buttons. "Where is it?"

"Hurry up! She's getting closer," Heather said as the shuffling sound got louder.

"I don't want to see that nightgown!" Emily said as she covered her eyes.

"For Pete's sake!" Jennifer shoved Emily out of the way and hit the *close door* button.

The cafetorium was crowded for the movie night showing of *Pearl Harbor*, which was projected onto the wall at the back of the stage. The girls sat on the couch by the air conditioner, and The General sat in a chair next to them with a big bowl of popcorn in his lap and a Floradora Flip in his hand. Afraid of dripping butter onto his uniform, he had several napkins tucked into the collar of his jacket.

"There!" Emily said as she pointed to the movie.

"Where?" The General asked.

"Holding the bandages."

"Are you sure this is the right scene?" Heather asked.

"I don't even see any women in this scene," Jennifer said. "Or kids."

"It's too far past now," Emily said. "Rewind it."

The General picked up the remote and started to rewind.

"Seventh time's the charm," Jennifer mumbled.

"There!" Emily yelled. "Three people to the right of Ben Affleck."

"Our right or his right?" Heather said.

"No one's right," Jennifer said. "*That's* Josh Hartnett."

"Too far again," Emily said.

As The General rewound, Helen approached the closed window behind the couch. Jennifer aggressively sat in front of it and said, "Are we really going to do this, Helen?"

"Can you turn it up?"

"What?" Jennifer said.

"The air conditioning."

"Turn it *up*?"

"It's pretty hot."

"What's up your sleeve, Helen?"

"Nothing. Martha and I are a little hot on the other side of the room. It's far from the unit, and we're knitting with all that wool yarn."

Jennifer looked over to Martha, who was wearing a similar knit scarf to the one that Helen was wearing and sitting under a pile of yarn. Jennifer looked back to Helen. "OK," she said carefully. "I'll turn it up."

"Thank you!" Helen returned to her seat next to Martha and picked up her knitting needles.

Wonders never cease! Jennifer thought. As she reached over to turn the knob on the AC, an unfamiliar woman in her forties approached and tried to open the window next to the unit. Jennifer quickly leaned in front of it. "Yes?"

"I want to open the window," the woman said. "This room needs fresh air."

"The air conditioning is on."

"And this room is filled with stale air. It's not healthy," the woman said. "I'm a holistic medical professional. I know what I'm talking about."

It took all of Jennifer's willpower to keep from rolling her eyes. "Who are you?"

"I'm Theresa. I just moved in."

"Since you're new, Theresa, you might not know that there are only a few public rooms at The Zonderling with air conditioning. This is one of them, so the windows need to stay closed to keep the cool air inside for everyone."

"Like I said, I'm in holistic medicine," Theresa said. "In my professional medical opinion, this window needs to be open for health reasons." Theresa reached for the window, but Jennifer wouldn't budge.

"Well, Theresa," Jennifer said. "It's a putrid steam bath of melting garbage outside. If you want to go sit in that healthy 'fresh air,' you should leave the room. Because I'm not letting you touch the window."

"I'm in medicine!"

"If you say so."

"Another self-absorbed millennial," Theresa scoffed. "All you can think about is yourself."

"How do you not understand the facts about opening a window?"

"How do you not understand the facts about fresh air?" Theresa said as she pulled a cigarette pack out of her pocket and removed a cigarette with her teeth.

The General immediately noticed the package of contraband. His contraband sensors were as sharp as the creases on his trousers. "Whoa, whoa!" The General said. "Theresa, you cannot smoke inside. You have to go on the sidewalk. The French girls can show you where to go."

Theresa rolled her eyes and left the cafetorium. Jennifer yelled, "Sorry, Gen X! Reality bites!"

"Stop rewinding!" Emily yelled. "There I am!"

"I still don't see you," The General said. "Maybe I should go get my field binoculars."

Heather and Jennifer exchanged glances. This was going to last forever until someone spotted Emily. Or pretended to.

"Oh, there you are!" Heather said. "Yeah, I see you! I can't believe I know someone in a movie!"

"Yes, right there!" Jennifer said. "Being in a movie. With the bandages. And Ben Affleck!"

"So cool right?" Emily said.

"So cool."

"Why can't I see you?" The General said.

"I'm the one holding the newspaper."

"Yeah, yeah," Heather said.

"The newspaper!" Jennifer said. She looked at Heather and shrugged.

"Oyster crackers!" The General said. "This is the most depressing thing since discovering that *P. Marshall* in the guest book is not Penny Marshall, despite all evidence to the contrary." The General grabbed a handful of popcorn. "Her restraining order made that pretty clear."

ACKNOWLEDGMENTS

I've been working on the idea for *The Zonderling* ever since I studied writing at the Upright Citizens Brigade Training Center in New York. The script that I wrote during the summer of 2010 was the first incarnation of what would become this book, so a big thank you to Jessica Stickles, who taught me all the basics of writing an original sitcom pilot.

I also want to thank my fab friends and family members, who have read countless drafts over the past five years, specifically the following:

Jeanne Bartow
Katie Buss
Lisa Cannavan
Joe Cristalli
Anne Lupardus Hanson
Erin Martin
Doug Niebruegge
Jayne Niebruegge
Mia Niebruegge
Matt Poreba
Sarah Williams

Thank you all for your feedback and endless support! Even Joe Cristalli, who prefaced his notes with this comment that makes me laugh every time I think about it: "This isn't supposed to sound like an insult, but you're pretty damn funny. Obviously, when we worked together, you were a total bore and nightmare, so you can understand why I'm surprised at your writing ability." (See what I mean about endless support?!)

Thanks for reading *The Zonderling!*

Kersti x

PS For those curious minds...*zonderling* is a funny-sounding word that means *eccentric* in Dutch.

ABOUT THE AUTHOR

Much like Tom Hanks in *Bosom Buddies*, or totally like Grace Kelly in real life, Kersti Niebruegge lived in old-fashioned residential hotels for women when she moved to New York City. She grew up in Wisconsin and graduated from the University of Wisconsin-Madison with a degree in journalism. Kersti has worked for BBC Worldwide, *Conan*, and *Late Night with Seth Meyers*. Her first book, *Mistake, Wisconsin*, is a satire about a fishing-obsessed small town in the Northwoods.

kerstiniebruegge.com
facebook.com/kerstiniebruegge
@kniebruegge

ALSO BY KERSTI NIEBRUEGGE

Mistake, Wisconsin

Deep in Wisconsin's eccentric Northwoods, a high school sophomore realizes she must take on a corrupt politician if she wants to save her town's beloved holiday—musky fishing Opening Day.

"...debut author Niebruegge creates a light, humorous mystery filled with Midwestern references—cheese curds, lutefisk dinners, supper clubs, and high school sports—and a touch of Northwoods folklore." — *Publishers Weekly*

"...small-town shenanigans, all things fishing, and teenage observations of everyday life with an appealing satirical tone..." — *Kirkus Reviews*

"...a deftly crafted Wisconsin culture based novel that demonstrates author Kersti Niebruegge's impressive storytelling talents..." — *Midwest Book Review*